"Sometimes, there are good reasons why some things are buried."

– Andrew Trumbull

"It's about time that someone showed the Tudors for the Philistines that they were."

– Emily Trumbull Ryan

"Fruitcakes should only be seen at Christmas."

– The author's mother

Cover photograph by Photographic Services,
Sittingbourne, Kent
Cover design by Bespoke Designs, Yelverton, Devonshire

ISBN: 979 8364 159854

Bickering

a novel by

Michael Reidy

Lattimer & Co.

PHILADELPHIA • PARIS

2023

a Nicola, l'incantevole signora
con la bicicletta

Every time I paint a portrait, I lose a friend.
John Singer Sargent

Foreword

This is the third outing for Sir Nigel and Sophie. After their first appearance in *On the Edge of Dreams and Nightmares*, I was surprised to find that they wanted further adventures, and these are described in *Circle of Vanity*.

Still, rather than retiring gracefully, they pestered me – in a way only other novelists will understand – to make one more appearance here.

There's a line in *The Jane Austen Book Club* where one of the characters, Sylvia Avila, says, "I just love the idea of characters having a secret life that the author doesn't even know about."

Although I never articulated it, I think this is something I always believed.

At university, we had endless debates on whether an author had the final word about the meaning of his books. While I never believed the pseudo-psychological claptrap that critics forced on novels, I did recognise that once a writer dies – and is no longer around to defend his work (or correct his mistaken readers) – the book enters a new phase of its existence and is subject to all manner of abuse and interpretation. For writers – and artists – of previous centuries about whom little is known anyway, their works have been forced to support even more ludicrous propositions.

I don't know what Sir Nigel, Sophie, Marissa and the others get up to outside these pages, but, as Jane Austen said, "It's only a novel."

August 2022
Saint Avit-Frandat

Bickering

Chapter One

$\mathscr{S}$ophie Gregg (stage name Ligeia Gordon – now Dame Ligeia) had recently finished a run in a West End comedy and was enjoying a break before rehearsals began in late May for a summer tourist run of *Relative Values*.

"It's going to be curious to see where the laughs come from on this one," she said to me, at the end of the meal. "I fear most of the humour will come from how dated the piece is, not how risqué."

Sophie and I had been friends for a very long time and lived in our own sets (or chambers) at Albany, in Piccadilly. Our close – but curious - relationship suited us, but only our closest friends understood. If anything characterised the relationship, it was Sophie's determination to push me out of my comfort zone. In return, I was Sophie's confidant and keeper of secrets.

On Friday nights, if neither of us was busy, Sophie would cook a steak with *frites* and garnishes. I'd provide a good bottle of wine – and gin, if needed.

While Sophie is a highly visible stage, radio and television actress, I am a portrait painter. A Royal Academician and active member of the Royal Society of Portrait Painters. I have painted the great and the good for forty years. While my paintings are recognised, I have

3

managed to keep a low profile. Apart from the odd prize, and my knighthood, the most publicity I have received has been through Sophie.

While Sophie's life is always changing, with productions and filming all over the country, my routine has been largely unchanged for forty years: I walk to my studio in Southwark every day, visiting a gallery or attending a lecture or concert, and dining at my club (or someone else's).

Sophie, not yet sixty, had, a decade before, commissioned me to paint her. During the sittings, she revealed that we had met before when she was fourteen and visiting her cousin at the Cambridge college where I had been doing a PhD in Mathematics.

She also revealed that she had murdered her uncle.

Although I never got to the bottom of that one, it seemed unlikely, as Sir Desmond's death was never considered anything but suicide.

Sophie cleared the table and shortly, odd noises began coming from the kitchen.

Puddings had never been Sophie's forte, but on this evening, the *crème brûlée* was nicely toasted rather than earlier attempts that had been truly Napoleonic in their scorched earth appearance.

I stayed out of Sophie's kitchen. First, because it was too small, and secondly, the idea of being in a confined space with Sophie wielding a blow torch is too far out of my comfort zone.

"This is very good," I said, with enjoyment.

"It's just something I threw together."

"Well, your aim is improving."

She put her spoon down with a clatter and glared at me.

I went on eating, not returning the glare.

Sophie sighed.

"All right," she said, just as the silence was becoming uncomfortable. "I wasn't going to spoil your weekend and wait until tomorrow night to tell you."

She gave a dramatic pause.

One of the problems with friendships with actors is that it's very difficult to tell when they are doing a bit from a scene or being genuine. Sophie didn't usually play games, so I looked up at her.

"April Gilliat called me today."

Another pause.

Sophie knew that I would not be pleased to hear anything from that family. April was an old Cambridge friend of Sophie's who lived on a farm in Lincolnshire. Not long after her husband died, she had contacted me about a portrait which I later discovered was to be of her eccentric daughter, Marissa, and not April herself.

The convoluted misunderstandings and the assumptions – supported by Marissa – that there was something

5

going on between us amused Sophie but horrified me. Marissa was thirty-seven, and I nearly twice that. I put it down to a manifestation of their recent bereavement and mild madness.

I was so uncomfortable about being with them that I shipped Marissa's portrait to Lincolnshire rather than drive it up as I would have usually done.

Sophie hadn't spoken any further, so I continued to enjoy my pudding while I could.

"April brought me up to date on everything since our last visit," she resumed, when I had put down my spoon.

"Marissa inherited everything," she continued. "April is well provided for and can live at Bickering Place as long as she wants, but it's Marissa's now."

"And what is *l'enfant terrible* up to now?" I asked.

"She's jacked in working as an estate agent, even though she passed her FRICS qualification before Christmas," Sophie said. "April says she's doing some archaeological work on the estate."

I remembered that Marissa had a degree in Arch and Anth and had mentioned a project during our sittings.

"On her own?"

"She's got a few friends helping, according to April. "Everyone gets lunch at Bickering Place."

"I suppose April's lucky they're not all camping there," I said. "Do you know the place where she's digging? Was it part of the priory?"

I didn't know much about Bickering. It wasn't far from Horncastle, but it no longer existed. There had been a small disreputable priory that had been passed back and forth between a number of orders – all remotely governed – until the dissolution. There had also been a large manor, Bickering Hall. Before my visit, I had tried to find pictures of it online, but only succeeded in finding two short mentions of it relating to rival Plantagenet and Tudor supporters. The hall doesn't appear to have warranted being painted or drawn and it was pulled down in the late 16th or early 17th century.

Bickering Place contained a gothic window – featured in my portrait of Marissa – that her father had found when ploughing. It was unclear whether it had come from the hall or the priory, but it fit well in its new home.

"April pointed to it as we drove by, but it was mostly hidden by a hill that blocked it from the road," Sophie said. "I just remember seeing part of a ruined rectangular brick building. I just remembered that it was brick. It might have been a barn or outbuilding.

"April mentioned that Marissa was fascinated by it, and by the lack of any other ruins of Bickering," she continued.

"The village was probably no more than some peasant hovels of the farm workers and domestic staff," I ventured. "After a few hundred years of ploughing, everything would be gone and the larger stones carted off and used elsewhere."

We moved from the table when Sophie served coffee and brandy. She sat on a period sofa that had come from the set of a production of *Private Lives* while I sat on a typically English heavily padded armchair covered with Chintz, possibly from the early days of Laura Ashley. At least it was comfortable.

"Anyway, April said she was bored with Marissa out of the house from dawn until dusk and suggested I come up as long as I was resting."

Sophie said this in a matter deliberately calculated to provoke me. I simply nodded and drank my coffee.

"Just don't get murdered in your bed."

Sophie gave me a cold stare, then smiled.

"She also said they'd both love you to come, too."

୫୦

After she had said that, Sophie began talking about a new play that she wanted to see, leaving me to stew over the suggestion.

I easily dismissed it. Sophie didn't bring it up again until Saturday when I cooked for her. Saturday night suppers were usually some form of pasta dish that I inexpertly made. I would never make it to *Masterchef*, but they usually tasted good and Sophie enjoyed them.

During the week, Bill and Virginia Warren visited London. Bill was a retired Scotland Yard chief inspector whom I had known since Cambridge. His wife, Virginia, had formed a close friendship with Sophie.

Bill and I did a lot of nothing while Virginia and Sophie went shopping. Though not a fan of galleries and museums, Bill and I passed the time easily in conversation and a stroll by some of London's lesser known curiosities, film locations, and sites of infamous crimes or the residences of their perpetrators.

I managed to steer him to the Wallace Collection, and though he didn't resist, he didn't look happy. He perked up when I ignored the Poussins, Fragonards and Vuillards and headed for the courtyard restaurant.

There, over lunch and a decent white Rioja, we exchanged stories of some of the dodgy characters we'd encountered in our work. Bill's clientele was more larcenous and murderous than mine, but having painted many aggressive bank executives and ambitious barristers, I was able to hold my own.

"There seems to be a point where otherwise ordinary people detach from reality," Bill said. "And, once they do that, they can do anything."

"Not seeing clearly can certainly create a world of illusions," I said.

Bill laughed.

"Isn't that what you do?"

He was right.

"Up to a point, Lord Copper. I try to synthesise appearance and personality," I said. "I have never deliberately tried to enhance the ego already present. I find that it expresses itself rather well anyway."

Bill considered this.

"I suppose, if someone is already over-inflated, it's difficult to add to it further," he said. "There are one or two of your more notorious sitters whose portraits today – given what we know about them now – seem to have had their criminal futures foreshadowed in their picture."

It was an observation that took me off guard. It took me back to when I painted Sophie for the first time. She had wanted a triple portrait that included objects from the plays she had been in. We'd settled on a skull, a raven and a candelabra. The skull related to several Shakespeares and also served as a *memento mori*, as in Holbein's *The Ambassadors*.

These had been selected before she'd told me about her abuse and her subsequent murder of her uncle.

What other clues had I inadvertently painted over the years? Objects placed in paintings are never there by accident. Some are simply favourite things, others references to present or past occupations, others are symbolic or emblematic. Most are chosen by those being painted, but I chose many others. Since I seldom keep in touch with sitters, unless they made the national newspapers, I had no way of knowing what undivulged crimes they may have committed.

"You'd be surprised to learn how many murders have been solved by the perpetrator having an emotional attachment to an object," Bill was saying when I began to concentrate again.

"Really?" I asked, trying to catch up. "That seems to be such a basic mistake."

Bill drank some of his wine and nodded.

"Classic example is in the old Hitchcock film. The mistress of the murderer keeps a piece of the murdered wife's jewellery which is recognised by the detective."

I was intrigued.

"Are some objects more frequently the giveaway than others?"

"Jewellery, artworks, and clothing seem to be the most popular," Bill replied. "The top one might be cash, but since it's hard to trace, we can't be sure."

"Clothing?"

"The common theme is envy. A good dress can be a powerful motive, though we did have someone we managed to convict who'd stolen an Armani tie."

I burst out laughing.

"Hard to believe," Bill conceded. "But, we've also had cars, stamps, coin collections, football and cricket memorabilia. . ."

"Not rugby or tennis?" I asked, sarcastically.

"No, almost never," he replied. "Footballers and cricketers are the most blood-thirsty."

℘

That evening, the four of us went out to dinner at an Indian restaurant near the Edgeware Road where a part-time actor that Sophie knew worked.

Anoushka ensured that we were spoiled, given larger portions, extra dishes and treats.

In spite of having lived in Britain for nearly forty years, Virginia had limited experience of Indian food.

"I've tried for decades to get Virginia to eat Indian food," Bill said. "Thank you, Sophie, for finally making it happen."

"You never told me it was this good!" Virginia retorted. "You just went to Indian restaurants for your long lunches and didn't bother to convince me."

"I begged you to go," Bill protested.

"I just think that if you're using that much spice, you're hiding something."

I thought the exchange had a bit of the ritual about it; it was hard to believe that anyone could live in England for as long as Virginia had and not have been to an Indian restaurant. However, their banter was amusing and something we'd not seen that often.

Sophie was laughing hard as she attempted to describe the various dishes to Virginia.

"It's delicious. I'll eat it, but I don't want to know about anything," Virginia exclaimed.

"Pity you can't get Bombay duck anymore," Bill said to me. "That would really get her going."

It was an easy evening, and when we were unable to consume anything more except some coffee, Sophie mentioned April's invitation.

"Are you going to go?" Virginia asked. "I didn't think Nigel liked her."

"He thinks they're both deranged," Sophie laughed.

"I've warned her to stay at a hotel," I said.

"Don't be silly," Virginia said. "When a friend invites you to stay, you stay with her."

"I'll probably be given the garden shed," Sophie said. "I think the house is full of Marissa's friends, the ones helping her with her dig."

Sophie gave details of what she thought the dig was and we speculated on how well she might manage it and how long it might take.

"The longer the better," I whispered to Bill. "It will keep her away from London."

I had told him about Marissa's affected infatuation with me and her erratic behaviour.

"As long as Sophie stays out of trouble and doesn't ask me to come up and rescue her, she should have a nice time," I said.

"You're getting stuffy again, Nigel," Sophie laughed. "Isn't it time you had another adventure?"

Chapter Two

Monday

I accompanied Sophie to King's Cross to help her with her luggage. On her third attempt, she managed to fit her clothes into one suitcase that she could manage without assistance.

She would have to change trains at Peterborough.

"There are lifts if you have to change platforms," I said.

She gave me one of her dirtiest looks.

"It's at times like that that my fans materialise and carry my baggage," she said, grandly.

"Yes, they carry it off and you never see it again."

"You're really pushing it today," she said, then smiled. "Keep it up and I'll make you come with me."

The platform was posted. I walked her to the barrier, handed over her suitcase – which she'd forgotten about – and kissed her goodbye.

"I'll email you all the gossip," she said, as she merged into the crowd.

◌ঙ

I took the Underground to London Bridge and walked to my studio. There was no sitting today, but projects in progress needed attention. Fortified with coffee, I worked through lunch until about three when I began to walk home.

On impulse, I called into Tate Modern. The works created for the Turbine Hall are sometimes amusing and often unexpectedly controversial. Artistically, they are seldom of any merit, but their often interactive element makes them entertaining.

An early installation (around 2003) was brilliantly atmospheric and engaging. Olafur Eliasson, an Icelandic-Danish artist, created a piece called *The Weather Project* which had a surprisingly realistic sunset that glowed with an intensity that attracted the eye. Its edges were as soft as Rothko's.

From the mezzanine, it was dazzling, but below was where the real fun was. The massive hall floor was bare and people wandered around looking up, or lay down to gaze at the wonderfully mirrored ceiling. One of the times I was there, a group of students was having fun making letters, words and shapes with their bodies and watching their reflections. Jets of artificial smoke appeared from time to time to add to the dusky effect.

Only after looking at the sun and studying its effect did one realise the superb illusion: only the bottom half of the sun was there; the top half was a reflection.

Like most such things, the explanation was bigger than the massive work itself; something that only diminishes both the work and the writer as far as I'm concerned.

Attracting more publicity was Ai Weiwei's *Sunflower Seeds*. About 1,600 workers in a Chinese village made and hand-painted a hundred million porcelain sunflower seeds and shipped them to England where they were spread on the floor of the Turbine Hall.

Visitors could lie on them, dig in them, walk on them and wonder at their number and realism.

That was until the Health & Safety mandarins closed the exhibition because the ceramic dust caused by walking or otherwise moving the seeds was deemed to be dangerous. This was particularly ironic as the hundred million seeds were supposed to be some sort of statement of honouring those who suffered under Mao Tse-tung.

The seeds were rearranged with a clear path around the porcelain and continued to attract visitors who seemed to enjoy it in spite of the bureaucrats and the blitherers of the art world.[1]

On my present visit, the Turbine Hall floor had blue lights shining on it. It may have been painted blue, too.

———

[1] In 2012, the Tate bought ten tons of the seeds (about eight million seeds) for an undisclosed amount. A year earlier, Sotheby's had auctioned a few bushels of them at about £ 3.50 per seed. Today, they sell on eBay for varying amounts, and no one can tell if they'd ever been near the Tate or Ai Weiwei. A fellow painter used to leave them as tips in restaurants for particularly bad waiters.

Various concealed projectors gave motion to the surface and the illusion of walking on water surprised me from time to time. The illusion of depth was convincing in several areas. Perhaps the floor was painted a deeper blue in these places, but there were no sharp lines.

The walls were painted with stylised California modern buildings and palm trees, giving the impression that one was drowning in a David Hockney. A diving board was attached to the end wall about two-thirds of the way up. There was the continuous noise of splashing and children laughing, calling and screaming at each other, and, occasionally, there would be a deeply resonating twang of the diving board, followed by a splash that dwarfed the others. Adding to the effect were periodic blasts of mist that would fall lightly on the crowd below.

By the time I left, I felt refreshed, just as after a trip to the Lido.

Total tosh as art, though.

I forwent the other galleries, having had my fill of faux art, and walked along the embankment to what I still thought of as Hungerford Bridge. The mass of tourist crowds hadn't yet arrived, but there were still large numbers who would drift from one side of the pavement to the other, suddenly stop, or turn, sideswiping the unwary with their backpacks.

Although I had done that walk – with slight variations – about ten thousand times, it remained interesting, passing, as it did many historical and popular tourist landmarks. I won't quote Doctor Johnson, as it's perfectly possible to be tired of London and *not* tired of life.

There's always Paris.

❧

I cooked for myself that evening as the club dining room was closed on Mondays. This was more by custom than any necessity as it had three chefs and plenty of other staff. The chefs also worked a few days a week in restaurants or other clubs. It was good training for the younger ones, and a way of keeping the more experienced ones from becoming stale. We benefitted from dishes stolen from the best restaurants in London – at a fraction of the price.

Once my salad was made and the lasagne in the oven (home, not ready-made), I settled down with a magazine and a Malbec.

Sophie regularly teased me when she saw my copies of *Philosophia Mathematica*, but I think she secretly liked that I still acknowledged that part of my life. The truth is that I need something to think about other than what paints I need to order, or how I can make a new sitter look good.

I had planned to go to the club for a drink with friends after supper, but hadn't finished the article on multiple infinities which postulated an infinity of infinities. (In a nutshell: there are an infinite number of points between the beginning and end of a one-inch line. Logically, there must be double that number between the beginning and end of a two-inch line, and so on.)

While of no scientific value whatsoever, I found such puzzles amusing. Intellectually, it was on a par with debates I had with one of the Farm Street Jesuits during which I suggested that God was an atheist. By the end of our discussion, he was quite taken with the idea.

So my evening passed. I don't go online or check emails often, I no longer have a television; I can see all I want on my laptop. Usually, I use it to find reference paintings, or to confirm the look of something.

This lack of regularly checking newsfeeds, Twitter, Instagram, TikTok, Snapchat and other purveyors of puerility meant that catching a glimpse of a headline the next day on the way to the studio was something of a shock.

I had called in at one of the newsagents on my route and while exchanging pleasantries with the shopkeeper, I saw a headline and photograph in the *Daily Express* that made me buy the paper for the first time.

"Singer Killed in Crash." Below the headline was a face I recognised.

American singer and fashion designer Fletcher Bailey, 30, and her manager, Jonathan Maitland, 43, were killed Saturday night when their car was struck by another vehicle in Los Angeles. The pair was thought to be returning to Beverly Hills following an informal dinner after a recording session. Details of the driver of the other vehicle were not available.

I had painted Fletcher Bailey – twice – several years ago while she was doing a UK concert tour. She was one of the seemingly bloodless gothic girls who were fashionable at the time.

When she first appeared with her manager, she seemed intimidated into silence. The girl herself was almost invisible behind layers of white powder, a double layer of false eyelashes, multiple blonde hair extensions and teetering in thigh-length platform boots. While the fans appeared to enjoy the performances, there were major mechanical or electronic failures that disappointed critics and social media opinionators so that when she and Maitland appeared at my studio, they were both edgy – at least while together.

Fletcher Bailey had surprised me when she later contacted me independently. She had seen a small oil sketch I had done of Sophie lying on the grass at Versailles and wanted a similar picture of herself, just for her. The picture was in a loose style so, unless you knew who it was, you wouldn't recognise her. This is what Miss Bailey wanted.

Unbeknownst to her manager, she visited my studio several times. She had taken an inordinate amount of time in the studio's bedroom preparing, and when she emerged, I could see why.

She had shed her public image and what came out was a small young lady in a simple short dress, flat shoes and the merest touch of makeup.

During those sittings, she said little, but seemed to be relaxed. When she spoke, her insecurity was still evident, but she was polite and very grateful when I delivered the final painting.

"This is for me," she repeated, when I showed it to her.

As for the main portrait, it was never finished. Before it was done, Miss Bailey had fallen after a performance, broken her ankle and returned to California.

Maitland later wrote that I could keep the deposit that had been made on the picture.

It was a mixed memory. I felt profoundly sorry for Fletcher Bailey during the time I spent with her. She seemed to have little life of her own. Just as music producers construct a band from people who had never met each other before, so Fletcher Bailey had been manufactured from a pliable little girl of meagre talent.

For all her hit records, she knew that the voice she heard wasn't hers but the product of skilful mixing, electronic beats, Auto-Tune, and other digital overproduction.

She seemed to get very little enjoyment from her success, fans or fortune.

I don't keep much from my sittings unless the sitter is particularly famous or likely to be. There would just be too many sketches (pencil and oil) to store, and none of it would earn me anything, unless I became destitute in my old age.

I had a good collection of photographs of my paintings (printed and digital) so my legacy was secure, but I disposed of the preliminary materials – most of it wasn't "right" so there was no point in keeping it.

I did keep all my sketches of Sophie, and, as it happened, of Fletcher Bailey. As the full portrait had never been completed, I lived in hope that she might return to London and want it finished.

I have a closet with fitted vertical slots to hold my works in progress. There are about a dozen slots and there are seldom more than five portraits on the go at any one time, so there is ample space. The other slots are occupied with either rejected portraits or unfinished ones.

Every painter or photographer has works that don't find favour with their subjects. The easiest thing to do is destroy them. Keep them, and they begin to haunt you. I usually wait a year in case there is a change of heart, or if some friend or relative wants to see it and acquire it. After that, out come the scissors.

The unfinished portrait of Fletcher was there, and I drew it out and placed it on the easel. Next, I located the sketchbooks that I'd used. They are lined up on bookshelves in date order with a list of the sitters on the cover.

I found that nearly five years had passed since she'd come to the studio. I looked at the sketches I'd done of her hands, eyes, ears, mouth and nose as well as the cursory sketches of what the portrait might look like.

The three of us agreed on a dramatic image with a full figure in her public black costume, walking towards the viewer. The background was conceived as two flat colours dividing the canvas diagonally. The lower right-hand triangle was black and the left was the same plum colour as her lipstick.

In the black section, her dress and form was invisible, being the same flat black as the background. This gave it a poster-like appearance that both Fletcher Bailey and Maitland liked.

At the time, I thought it might lead to more celebrity commissions, but alas.

Chapter Three

Tuesday

When Sophie telephoned that evening, I didn't mention Fletcher Bailey as our encounter had coincided with a period that I was displeased with her. Readers of *On the Edge of Dreams and Nightmares* will remember that at that time, following an incident with the paparazzi and the ensuing publicity, I distanced myself from Sophie (or more accurately, Ligeia Gordon) for several months.

We got over it, but the period was still tender.

"It's lovely up here," Sophie said, enthusiastically. "April is in her element, cooking lunch for the dig gang every day and revelling in listening to their conversation. I've not been down to inspect the site yet, but they've been at it for two days and are enthusiastic.

"Your portrait of Marissa looks so elegant next to the gothic window," she continued. "You really should come see it – in fact, you might just have the chance."

There was giggling and fumbling with the phone and I heard Sophie giggle.

"Sir Nigel, it's Marissa."

I wanted to feign line trouble and break the connection, but I knew Sophie would just call back.

"I've got a proposition for you," she said.

"*Marissa!*" I heard April shout.

"It's all right, I called him Sir Nigel," Marissa retorted.

"A proposition, Miss Gilliat?"

There was the beat of a pause as she debated whether to reply to the formality. I guessed that she didn't want to be diverted from her purpose, and her formality with me justified my response, but who knew what went on in that young lady's head?

"I'd like to commission you to come up and draw sketches of the dig and maybe develop one or two into paintings," she said.

"I – "

"Sophie thinks it's a brilliant idea. I'll get you the same room at the Captain John Smith. Can you come up next week? The weather's supposed to be good, and I think Sophie misses you."

This time, it was Sophie's turn to protest, but all I heard was the three of them giggling.

ಲ

Wednesday

After a normal day, during which I was able to put Marissa and her mother out of my mind, I returned to my set, read my post, put supper in the oven, switched on my laptop and poured a glass of Fitou.

Checking my emails, I found I had one from Marissa, which I chose to read last.

Dear Sir Nigel,

You will gather that we're having a good time with a houseful of people and Sophie, but the dig is serious, and I would very much like you to do a series of sketches. Perhaps watercolours. I think they would be an excellent addition to Bickering Place and an additional piece of documentation of the dig.

Sod's law, it started raining this evening and is set to continue for a few days. With luck, things will have time to dry out over the weekend.

If you could come next Tuesday we will be close to being finished clearing the area of overgrowth and modern debris.

She went on to propose a figure to cover four days, three nights at the hotel and car hire. Although already tempted, it was her professional sign-off that persuaded me that she was serious.

Before going to the studio the next morning, I sent a holding email to Marissa saying that I would look at my schedule and get back to her soon. A Tuesday departure would give me good preparation time, and I needed to check my supplies of ink and watercolours. Since I didn't use them regularly, I had no sense of what I might need.

At the studio, Thursday, I made a short list of what I might need. I had to arrange a car big enough to accommodate my clobber.

That evening, I was reviewing my list of things to do and buy when Sophie called.

"Sorry about the other night," she began. "We'd had a very good dinner."

"You were like school girls making prank calls," I scolded.

"Yes, I'm sorry."

"I did have a sensible email from Marissa which has given this archaeological expedition a better chance – but architectural sketches and watercolours aren't — "

"Nigel," Sophie interrupted, urgently, "there's something else I think you'd better get up to see. Maybe several things."

"A body in the library?"

"Nigel, I'm serious," she said. "Meet us at the site when you come – I'll email you a map and directions. I'll have a pair of Wellies for you as there's a lot of dirt around. I'll fill you in once you're here."

"Watercolours aren't my thing – " I began to protest.

"Nonsense! The ones you did for me in Paris are wonderful."

It was pointless to argue.

"Do I need to bring anything special?" I asked.

"Just your wits – and your usual inspection kit."

I emailed Marissa to say I'd meet her at the site late Tuesday morning. Sophie sent me directions and a scan of a map which I printed. She also attached a few photographs she'd taken.

Looking at the map, I'd driven past the site several times on my previous visit.

I had a light lunch at a wine bar near the studio and then went paint shopping. There are some wonderful small shops in the area, and I was able to top up my supplies of masking tape, masking fluid and additional rolls of paper towels as well as a few tubes of colour.

I even managed to work a few hours before walking to the Boot & Flogger for dinner where I'd arranged to meet an old friend whom I hadn't seen for a few years.

℘

Thursday evening

David Powell was one of those people who one stays in touch with because of a distant shared experience. In this case, it was judging a competition of student art in Kent and Sussex. Powell lived in Sussex which is why he had been enlisted, and I was roped in because I had just painted the leader of Kent County Council. The other judge on that occasion had been the curator of Parham House.

While the three of us had, at least on paper, impressive credentials, the fact was that we had no idea whatever of how to judge art by school children, ranging in age from 7 to 18.

Powell suggested a solution. Each of us would independently walk through the exhibition, of more than a thousand entries, and then gather for a coffee to discuss initial impressions.

"Once we've seen what's there, we can make up some criteria for judging," he proposed, and we accepted.

Although a lengthy process, it produced results that we were happy with and, surprisingly, the organisers.

Powell and I met long after that when he came to see the Summer Exhibition of the Royal Society of Portrait Painters. He subsequently gave one of my entries a favourable mention. I put this down to the fact that I had paid for lunch.

At that time, he was just beginning to look into the death of a friend of his in a terrorist bombing in Greece. He very nearly got himself blown up in Athens in the process.

It was serendipitous that Powell had contacted me suggesting lunch. I suspect he doesn't come up from deepest Sussex often these days.

Powell was an art writer. Like the late, great Brian Sewell, he made no claim to being a critic. While I'd personally felt that Sewell was the greater expert, I found Powell's commentaries knowledgeable, his comments astute, and his eye for obscure detail remarkable. In certain areas of art history, he was as good as the best.

I found him at a table with a schooner of sherry looking at the food menu.

"The British never really appreciated sherry," he said, as I approached the table. "A bottle gets opened at Christmas, a few glasses are drunk with Grandma, and the bottle goes on the shelf until Easter when it might be finished. In Spain, it's treated like any other bottle of wine: you open it and drink it all."

He took another swallow, then stood up.

"It's good to see you, Nigel!" he exclaimed. "It feels like a decade has gone by. All the lockdowns and enforced hermitage have made me feel old."

We shook hands and took our seats.

"I know just what you mean," I said. "Finding the will to do anything is difficult."

The waiter came and I ordered a schooner of Sercial, just to be contrary.

"Does anything particular bring you to London?" I asked.

"Time to see the galleries again," he replied, before adding, "and a trip to my publisher."

"Ah! You didn't waste the last two years!" I said. "You were never one to be idle. What's the topic this time?"

"You know around the time I got married, I wrote a book about Islamic art?"

"I still have my copy," I said. "It was a fascinating book that skated nicely between its appeal to the scholarly and the general public. The idea of adding a chapter showing readers how they could create patterns for themselves was inspired. I think there are bathroom and conservatory floors all over the kingdom that can trace their inspiration to your book."

Powell laughed.

"The inspiration wasn't mine," he admitted, "it was Madeline's."

Madeline was the sister of Powell's BBC friend who had been killed. Up until his death, she'd been an entrepreneur who built an empire of High Street fashion stores, and immediately after her brother's death, sold it. Madeline must have netted tens of millions of pounds, yet, when she married Powell, she moved in with him in a small cottage, miles from a station.

"Will you be in London long?" I asked.

"A few days. Madeline will be coming up tomorrow."

"So, you're seeing your inappropriate friends today."

It was nearly impossible to bait Powell, and he gave no reaction.

"Actually, I was hoping I could tempt you to do some writing," he said, as the waiter arrived to take our orders.

It took me a moment to refocus on the menu. Powell was a writer of note. Well-known and admired, though not a media tart, he appeared enough so that his recognition was high.

When the waiter left, I retreated to my Sercial, but Powell pushed ahead.

"Your article on *The Picture of Dorian Gray* was quite a piece," he said, "even if few people fully understood what you were saying."

I had written "Picture or Portrait" (an essentially facetious commentary on the pretentiousness of ninety-nine percent of art criticism) for my own amusement and on a whim sent it to an art magazine that published it.[1] Unfortunately, the editorial staff failed to see it was a parody, pretty much proving my point.

"Our indiscretions always come back to haunt us," I replied.

Powell smiled easily.

"The publisher of the Islamic art book wants to publish a book of what they think are my best articles along with some new ones," he explained. "I can't think why. I've been feeling like a broken record for a decade and can't think anyone wants to read more."

I laughed. We'd re-established our footing and the ease of our relationship. If anything about him had changed, I reckoned it was married life that had done it.

---

[1] This article raised the silly question, "Why wasn't Wilde's novel called *The Portrait of Dorian Gray* rather than the *Picture of Dorian Gray*?" *Grosvenor Magazine*, CIV, No. 3, June 2019.

Madeline had made him more tolerant. I suppose Sophie had that effect on me, but less so.

"What do you want me to say?" I asked. "I can't think I have anything to add to your experience."

Powell contemplated the last of his sherry before drinking it.

"I think your adventure with the *Storm on the Sea of Galilee* outdoes most of my experiences," he said, giving me a knowing smile.

I was surprised he knew of it. Not many people did. Two years earlier, I had found myself involved with the authentication of a version of Rembrandt's missing masterpiece and had concluded that it was an extremely clever forgery.

Since the fraud involved other paintings, it was hushed up, and a number of the players retired.

"I can't write about that," I said, in a whisper.

"I'll send you the articles that are to be reprinted and the new ones when the publisher gives them the okay," he said.

I hadn't heard myself agree to any of this, but that didn't seem to matter.

"The whole thing won't need to be ready for about ten months, though you'll have to do an outline and a draft or two," Powell added.

"So it can be censored?"

He laughed.

"Not at all," he said, still laughing. "We just want something that will be a good fit with the topics I write about in the book. Nothing sycophantic. I don't think either of us minds a bit of controversy at our age."

I considered this.

"I should be able to do that," I said. "It might be fun."

"Let's make it fun," Powell said, extending his hand. "Something around five thousand words should do. Not too long, but enough to explore a few topics thoroughly. If the subject demands it, write more."

I had been thinking in terms of about fifteen hundred words, max. This was the length of a serious university essay.

The waiter arrived with our food, but my appetite had diminished.

Chapter Four

Tuesday

The morning went as planned. The car was delivered to my studio on time and I was able to set off before the traffic became too heavy. I wasn't fond of driving, but it didn't frighten me. I also liked more scenic routes and would take them if the time allowed.

Once out of London, I was able to consider Powell's proposition. We'd talked about it over our meal, and I was feeling happier by the time we'd finished. I could divide it into parts, in effect, writing two two-thousand word pieces with a bit left over. Given the topics he said would be included, it shouldn't be too daunting. Sophie could give me advice about my prose and would keep me from sounding too pompous.

I'd allowed time to stop for breakfast, and by prior arrangement, when I arrived in Horncastle, the Captain John Smith allowed me to take immediate possession of my room where I could refresh myself before heading to the site at Bickering.

෪

Sophie's map took me right to the site. It was about a mile from Bickering Place on a lane that appeared to follow ancient land boundaries. A few cars were pulled off the road in front of what must have been one of the only hills in that part of Lincolnshire. Even so, it was only about ten feet tall and resembled a barrow made to appear higher by undergrowth. A dirt road went straight over the top of it.

I left my materials in the car and walked up the hill to see what I could see.

What I saw was more endlessly flat Lincolnshire fields punctuated with hedgerows, the odd building and tree and before me, a brick ruin, mostly covered with vines. There were a few SUVs parked at the side. About a hundred fifty feet from the bottom of the mound was a building that was – or had been – rectangular with the remains of four windows on the side facing me. The walls were barely half their former presumed height, though at the corners, they reached up to what appeared to be nearly their full height.

It looked like the windows had been bricked up at one point. The change of use or the window tax were the most likely reasons.

I speculated on its age and original use, but remembered that I was only there to draw what I saw and nothing else. I continued to study the building, but eventually realised it was a stalling tactic and that there was no point in putting off seeing Marissa again.

I descended the hill and walked around the end of the building which had a large barn door-sized opening in it.

I could see about half a dozen people pulling down vines and cutting brambles. They had cleared about two-thirds of the area down to the ground and much of the internal walls. Actual excavation had yet to begin.

Sophie spotted me first and, looking up from her pruning, waved and came towards me. She, like just about everyone else, was wearing a Barbour and wellies. She wore virtually no makeup, and her hair blew around her face.

She gave me a hug and kissed my cheeks and hugged me again.

"Come join the fun!" she exclaimed. "Marissa, Nigel's here."

Marissa came from behind the large pile of cuttings and gave a big smile. Even in her flat boots, she looked taller than I'd remembered. She wore jeans and a maroon sweater under her jacket. She took off her work gloves as she approached, and shook her rich red hair, now even longer than it had been when I painted her.

She unashamedly took the final steps quickly, propelling herself into me and wrapping her arms around me.

"It's so good to see you, darling!" she giggled, and rested her head on my chest. "I didn't think you'd come."

When she finally stepped back, I glanced at Sophie who was holding her hand in front of her mouth to conceal her laughter.

"This is it," Marissa said, waving her arm over the scene. "Come into the car and I'll fill you in on what we're doing and get you a pair of wellies."

Her manner was now business-like, and I followed her to the Range Rover Defender parked at the front of the building.

"When the weather's more predictable, I'll set up a table for the maps, photographs and site records."

As it was, the vehicle was serving as an office and there were maps and papers piled high on the back floor and seats.

"This is what we know," she said, reaching for an A4 cloth-bound notebook.

She opened the book and began reading down the first handwritten page.

"This building first appears on maps from about the reign of Queen Anne. It's marked only as 'Bickering Hall (ruins of)'."

She turned the page and showed me a photocopy of the section of the map that showed it. Beneath it, she'd written, c. 1705.

"Bickering, or Bickering Hall, appears to have been demolished in the late fifteen hundreds, along with the small priory that was across the street.

"My first guess was that this was either part of the village that grew up around the hall, or possibly an out building."

I nodded.

"However, once we started stripping the vines and brambles off it, it appears to be later," she explained.

"The windows," I said.

Marissa nodded.

"And the bricks," she said. "It's hard to tell, but this could have been built in the first part of the seventeenth century. The window fillers are Tudor brick which were probably from other buildings."

She reached into the back seat and produced a Tudor brick and handed it to me.

"Unmistakeable," she said. "The older bricks are thinner and slightly shorter than later ones which tend to have a length that's twice the width."

"Is that true?" I asked, fascinated to learn something new and so obvious.

"Not one hundred percent of the time, but it's a good guideline."

She dropped the brick back on the rear floor and showed me the next page of the book.

"The goals for the dig are simple," she continued. "Clear and stabilise the site; determine its prior uses; and, decide whether it can be restored or developed.

"We're working with the county planners and archaeologists, though they are not taking part in the dig. They'll show up every now and then to see how we're getting on," Marissa explained. "I don't think they believe this is an important enough site to waste too much time on."

"Do you think it is?"

Marissa closed the book and leaned back in the driver's seat and stared straight ahead.

"I always wanted to do something that used my archaeology and anthropology degree. Father didn't want me to study that. He wanted me to do land economy."

"Hence your work as an estate agent," I said.

"Yes. He wanted me to be able to take over from the farm agent when he – the agent – retired. He's a good agent, and he and I worked closely for a year or so, so I know every corner of the land, the rotations, the drainage, fertilisers – everything," she said. "I'd done enough in my real job to develop a good understanding of property, and I picked up a lot from my father growing up here."

She turned more pages in the book. There were photocopied pages relating to Bickering Hall and Bickering Priory, Ordnance Survey maps of various ages, and a number of old sketch maps.

"Lincolnshire was a very mixed county in the late Plantagenet and Tudor periods. That meant that it was also pretty mixed as far as Catholics and Protestants, too," Marissa said. "Buildings were destroyed, rebuilt, repurposed and so on for three hundred years."

While interesting, this wasn't why I was here, and with each page turn, Marissa was leaning closer to me.

"What do you want me to do?" I asked.

Before setting her book aside, she pulled out a few loose sheets and handed them to me.

There was a list of nearly two dozen possible pictures with pencil sketches next to each to show from where I could see the scene, and a small sketch of the scene itself.

Before I could comment, Marissa resumed.

"Since we haven't uncovered anything yet, this will change, but it will give you an idea of what I'm after," she explained. "These angles should give a good view of the trenches we're planning. Others show the building when cleared. We are planning to remove the old brick from the windows. Depending on what we find – for example, any decorative pieces in the rubble – I might ask you to work with one of the team to develop a painting of what the building might have been.

"While I want watercolours that can be framed and hung, the prime purpose is to record the dig," she said.

I read the "shoot list."

"Aerial views?"

She gave a smile. "We have a drone. Something might turn up from that view – something the camera captures, something revealed by the light."

I nodded. This was very thorough.

"Do you want people working in the pictures?" I asked.

This appeared not to have occurred to her before.

"About half," she said.

"Half the people or half the pictures?"

She gave a big smile.

"You always make me laugh, darling," she said. "I'll leave that to you – but they mustn't all be of Sophie."

so

By the time the briefing was finished, the team was taking a coffee break. What I was expected to do had expanded considerably, but Marissa quickly agreed a pro rata rate on the additional work – but I still only had until Friday to complete enough of the work that could be finished back in London.

Sophie passed me a mug of coffee.

"Still alive with your honour intact?" she asked, impishly.

"Has anything been found yet?" I asked, leaving that bit of bait alone.

"Didn't she tell you? What did you do in that car all that time? I bet the windows were steamed up by the time you got out."

She could barely contain her laughter and loved seeing my irritation.

"*Sophie!*" I whispered, sharply.

She continued to giggle for a minute then grew serious.

"Well, whatever you're feeling, it's a lot better than he is," she nodded to a young man, about Marissa's age, who was stirring his coffee. "That's Hillyard, a portrait of unrequited love.

"Max was on the same course as Marissa at Cambridge and was besotted with her then and still is. Apparently, he's a good archaeologist and gave up a stint in the American Southwest to come here."

"Wise man."

Sophie shot me a look but said nothing.

"Marissa asked him to head the dig," Sophie continued. "A few of the workers are his friends, a few Marissa's, and a few farm workers until they're needed for their normal work.

"He's a nice chap, good to work with and very helpful in explaining how to do things. I think he's quite clever, too. If he weren't running things, I don't think I would have encouraged you to come up."

She paused, considering her next words.

"But Marissa's using him?" I suggested.

She thought about this.

"On one level, yes, but she's not mean to him. From what I've seen, she respects his ability – and likes him – but I've not seen anything to show that she's leading him on. Poor boy."

It was a typical Sophie observation. Having known extreme emotional pain, she was sensitive to it in others.

"Introduce yourself," Sophie suggested. "I think you'll like him."

I began to step away.

"I don't think he knows that you're 'the other man,' but I'm not sure."

ର

After a few minutes talking to Max, I concurred with Sophie's assessment. He was intelligent, he seemed to have a very clear idea what he was doing and how to do it, and his eyes widened at every mention of Marissa.

We walked up the small hill as we chatted. At the top, I could take the time to evaluate the site and the surrounding landscape.

"As you know, Marissa invited me to do some sketches and watercolours of the dig," I began.

He nodded, indicating that he was aware of this.

"You did the portrait, didn't you?"

"Yes."

"It must have been nearly impossible to get her to keep still long enough to do it," he said, with a laugh.

"She gave me a list of set-ups," I said, borrowing the term from the photographers. "Perhaps we can go through them sometime and you can tell me where I won't be in your way. I have only until the end of the week to make the sketches. I can finish them at the studio."

He nodded.

"That sounds good."

"While we're up here, can you give me some context for this building?" I asked.

He took the binder he was carrying and opened it to a sketch map.

"You see, there's the building," he pointed to the map, "and behind us is this road. Then, over in that field to the left," he indicated an area across the road, "was the priory, and a few hundred metres to the right was Bickering Hall. What there was of any village would have been behind the dig."

He drew an arc with his hand that took in much of the surrounding area.

"I suspect they were just farm cottages, out buildings, and possibly some buildings associated with the priory and the hall: animal enclosures, sheds, grain storage, a dovecot, bee hives, maybe an extra guest house.

"The priory was always fairly small – no great church, library, school or hospital, though they probably had all of those things but in one or two rooms."

We began walking down the hill and back to the building.

"Do you know where the window was found that's in Bickering Place?" I asked.

Max laughed.

"That's about as confused as all the ancient stuff," he said. "Marissa says it was in that field behind the dig, and April says it was in the field across the road between the hall and the priory."

We re-entered the building. Max looked at his watch. It had just gone eleven-twenty.

"We can talk more over lunch. We'll go up to Bickering Place at one, and you and I and Marissa can review some of the history," he said, then turned towards the team.

"All right, everyone. Great progress this morning. Can we aim to have the brush all cleared by the end of the day?"

Marissa collected the coffee cups, biscuits and thermoses, put them in a basket and, presumably, took them back to her car.

Sophie handed me a pair of gloves and some secateurs.

"Until you start your real work, you might as well make yourself useful."

Chapter Five

Tuesday

Cutting brambles and clearing them from old walls, revealing bricks and stones that no one had looked at for a hundred – maybe two hundred – years was fascinating. After a few moments, I didn't feel the cold and struck a steady rhythm that I could sustain.

Sophie worked next to me silently, and in the time before lunch, we cleared a good section of ground and wall.

One of the other workers, a local chap called Stephen, whom I presumed worked on the farm, followed several of us, digging out bramble roots and carting brush away in a wheelbarrow. He told us that he'd burn it after we'd left for the day.

The roots of some of the invasive plants – buddleia, sumac, even wisteria as well as vines and brambles – were thick and needed considerable effort to be dislodged.

During one of our pauses, Sophie asked if I'd take her for supper that night.

"Make it early. We'll both be pretty tired," she said.

"What time do they knock off here?" I asked.

"Around five."

"Come to the hotel at seven," I said.

"Make it six-thirty and you can buy me a drink, too."

We resumed work and, as happens on such tasks, all of a sudden the end was in sight. We wouldn't finish clearing the interior of the building before lunch, but by the end of the day, it would be done, and possibly the remaining exterior walls.

At twelve-thirty, Marissa blew a whistle and everyone returned their tools to Max who had several large heavy-duty plastic trunks in the back of his SUV. We piled into our cars and drove to Bickering Place.

Sophie had come with Marissa but got into my car for the short ride.

I hadn't been there since painting Marissa's portrait. My experiences in Bickering Place were – what? unusual? bizarre? – let's say *curious*.

It had been not long after Titus Gilliat died and both April and Marissa were displaying an uneasy relationship, and Marissa had been unexpectedly – and inconsistently – flirtatious. In spite of that, I had managed to produce a prize-winning portrait.

"Nervous?" Sophie asked, as we turned onto the lane leading to the house.

"Are you surprised?"

"You have me with you this time. I won't let Marissa attack you," she giggled.

Our cars formed a veritable convoy, but the broad sweep before Bickering Place absorbed us all, though we were parked bumper to bumper.

April Gilliat stood at the front door waving everyone to the back where boots could be washed and taken off. She'd also put out an old laundry tub filled with hot water for a communal washing of the hands. Once satisfied that we weren't going to drop clods of mud everywhere, we were admitted to the house.

All this was done with a good deal of laughter and banter, and everyone accepted the ritual as a necessary one.

Inside, there were chairs dotted about the kitchen and a selection of food laid out on the table. Several large pots of stew were on the Aga and we grabbed plates and bowls, cutlery and bread.

I had just collected mine and was looking for a chair when Marissa appeared at my side.

"Come into the conservatory," she whispered in my ear.

I followed her into the hallway and stopped before her portrait which hung where I'd suggested. She continued into the conservatory and I followed, but returned to the hallway once I put my plate down.

"Do you like it any better?" I asked.

She gave me an uncomprehending look.

"The first time you saw it, you shouted at me and ran out of my studio," I reminded her.

"Yes, but the second time, I kissed you," she said, and stepped forward to do it again.

Of course, Sophie had chosen that moment to walk through the door, holding a glass of wine.

"Just in time, I see," she said, glaring at me. "Now come, Marissa, and let me rescue you from that notorious old *roué*."

I followed them into the conservatory and began my lunch while Sophie chatted about the morning's work.

"We've got the right amount of people today," Marissa said. "Enough to cut the brush and enough to carry it out and burn it. I think Max is pleased, too."

As if on cue, Max came in juggling his plate of stew and bread and a bottle of beer.

Sophie smiled at him.

"We were just saying how well we thought the morning went," Sophie said.

Max glanced at Marissa for confirmation. I could see none.

"It was a good morning," he said, more interested in eating.

"Do you have any idea what the building was?" I asked. "It hardly looks agricultural with all those windows."

Max waited to see if Marissa was going to say anything, but she'd resumed chatting to Sophie.

"It appears to have been a hall of some sort," he said. "It could have been used as a village hall, or maybe one of the owners of Bickering didn't want people in his house."

"Does it not post-date the destruction of Bickering Hall?"

"There is that," Max conceded. "It may have been a replacement family house."

"The maps don't show much," I said.

"No, they don't," he laughed, starting to become convinced that I knew a little about the site.

"One of the stories is that the mound in front of the site was built and planted with trees to hide Bickering Hall, and the village itself," Max said. "There well may have been trees six or a dozen deep along the road. All anyone would have seen would have been the priory on the other side of the road."

"Why the camouflage?"

"Yorkists and Lancastrians; Plantagenets and Tudors; Roundheads and Cavaliers; Protestants and Catholics. Who knows? They were always bickering about something around here."

೧೫

"Marissa's a bit hard on him, don't you think?" I asked Sophie in the car on the way back to the site.

"He'd stand a better chance if he just grabbed her, took her in his arms and kissed her," she replied.

I was shocked by this, not because of any feminist sensibilities, but because of Sophie's own experience of abuse.

As was her custom when I expressed shock, Sophie responded with laughter.

"It's not what I'd recommend for every woman, but Marissa needs to be woken up," she said. "Max has adored her for years and she has treated him indifferently at best. He'd do anything for her. He's nice, hardworking, and very good at his job.

"He's even more uneasy now that she's inherited Bickering Place, the farm and the money."

I considered this.

"So, she's even more unattainable. Pity."

"I'm less sympathetic," Sophie said. "I don't think she's paying attention to anyone. Until she stops wasting time trying to kiss you in dark corners and gets rid of her fixation on older men, she's not going to get anywhere. She's going to be thirty-nine in May and she appears not to be hearing her clock ticking."

I was silent as we approached the site. I parked and started to get out of the car, but Sophie remained still.

"What?" I asked.

"Well?" she demanded.

After a moment, I replied, "It wasn't a dark corner. It was the main hallway," and collected my materials and slammed the door.

৪১

With Max's approval, I set up my director's chair and materials. I then took pictures of the work in progress. I wanted to capture all the invasive growth before it was gone. This included what remained at the back of the building.

I opened the first of the half-dozen sketch pads I'd brought and set to work on the first of the requested images.

As with such things, as I neared the end of the first drawing, how to handle an aspect of it came to mind, and I began the second. I worked without break except to fetch my thermos of tea until, at four-thirty, the interior of the building was clear.

Sitting where I was, to the right of the doorway, I noticed for the first time that there was no window in the end wall.

"Max!" I called.

He was talking to Marissa, presumably about whether to call an end to the work for the day, which he did before coming over to me.

I stood next to him and we surveyed the full interior. The feeling of space and proportion was beginning to speak.

"Sit in my chair, Max," I said. "Close your eyes for a moment and then open them."

He did so.

"What do you feel – not see – but *feel*?"

"Good God!" he whispered.

"Indeed."

"It feels like a church!"

"It certainly feels that way," I said. "I leave it to you to make sense of the date as to what it might have been."

He regarded me.

"You have a suspicion?"

"I do, but I don't want to prejudice you," I said. "You have the historical evidence, I don't."

The site was nearly empty now.

While we were talking, Sophie had motioned to me that she'd be going back to Bickering Place with Marissa.

Max and I walked around, looking at the windows and walls in silence. It wasn't until we'd completed our circuit and were back at the front door that Max spoke.

"Tomorrow, half the team will finish clearing the outside of the building and the rest of us will begin excavating the floor," he said.

"Do you think there is a floor?" I asked.

"I pushed a probe down in a few places and hit something," he said. "We'll just have to see."

He paused, then said.

"Can you keep your suspicions about this building quiet for the moment?"

Chapter Six

Tuesday

Sophie had borrowed April's car and arrived at the Captain John Smith at exactly six-thirty, looking her more usual elegant self. I was already in the bar enjoying a gin and tonic.

"Funny that you couldn't wait for a drink when all you did was sit around all afternoon," she said as she sat down.

"And you didn't have a drink with a nibble or two with April?" I asked.

"That's beside the point," she said. "How did you get on? You were in deep conversation with Max when I left."

"We were talking about the best place for me to sit for tomorrow's work," I said. "He wants to start digging for the floor."

Sophie laughed.

"I can see it! you sitting on an island while the rest of the floor is excavated around you!"

"Unfortunately, Max didn't like that idea," I said. "I'll do a sketch of the empty space from the same place I drew the first one today, then move to the outside of the building," I said. "I've got photographs of everything, so I can cheat."

Sophie's drink arrived along with fresh bowls of nuts and olives. (I say "bowls" but if they were capable of holding more than ten olives, I'd like to see it.)

"Here's to tomorrow when the real work starts," Sophie said, raising her glass.

"I have all my pencils sharpened," I said. "Do you know what you'll be doing?"

"Marissa and Max dished out the jobs to those who are staying at Bickering Place," she said. "There will be two people digging, and six of us sifting the earth – three with coarse screens and three with finer ones."

"That's pretty labour intensive," I said. "The earth is dug, it's lifted again for the first screen, again for the second, and again for disposal."

"It's no worse than a supermarket," Sophie replied. "Every item is lifted six times."

"I didn't realise your knowledge of supermarkets was that great."

"I've opened enough of them," Sophie laughed. "No, I have to confess that nugget was from a play."

"That's a lot of earth even if the floor is only a foot down."

We drank and nibbled.

"You said there was something you wanted me to see at Bickering Place," I prompted.

"Mmm," she said, swallowing. "It may be nothing, but I thought it might be interesting.

"My room is in the attic – "

"Did you behave so badly while you were there before that you were banished?"

"I don't think it was that," she said. "There are a lot of people there and we're sleeping where we can. It's not an attic. They are servants rooms and, though small, are comfortable enough. There's only one bathroom up there, so some of us are allowed to use one on the first floor."

"Are you in that inner circle?"

"Yes."

She finished her drink.

"Let's eat," she said, standing up. "I need something to keep me warm tomorrow."

"The Italian around the corner?"

"Perfect."

CB

"*Five thousand words?!*" Sophie exclaimed, in the too-quiet restaurant over coffee. "Are you out of your mind?

"Have you ever written anything that length before?" she demanded.

"Not about art."

"I don't know how you survived all these years. It seems that you'll do anything for anyone."

She was clearly enjoying herself, and her *antipasti*, a good *lasagne, zabaglione* and half a bottle of decent

Chianti had primed her. Her coffee and *limoncello* launched her into action.

"David Powell is an established writer. What are you doing writing for *him*?" she demanded. "What made him ask *you*?"

I was taken aback and laughed in self-defence.

"Why does this bother you so much?" I asked.

Sophie sat back, took a deep breath and collected herself.

"Nigel, you're a *painter*. It's what you love and what you do best," she said. "I don't want to be morbid, but how many portraits do you think you have left in you?"

I knew what she was saying. I was at the stage of my life when people came to me because they wanted me to paint them before I died. Many great painters lived to ripe old ages and kept going. Others became visibly bored and the work declined, though no one ever says so.

In 1973, I went to the exhibition of the last two hundred or so Picasso paintings. It was fittingly – or ironically – at the *Palais des Papes* in Avignon. I still have the catalogue. I remember being shocked by the condition of the paintings. They showed signs of damage: distortions in the canvas, smeared paint, and broken stretchers. One could just imagine a bored Picasso spending fifteen minutes on one and then flinging the canvas across the room where it smashed against the wall, or hit another canvas.

The Picasso touch was still there, but not much of the inspiration.

Of course, you will read nonsense about how he was breaking new ground until the end, but deliberating honestly on these final paintings, even an amateur can see the truth.

I still win one or two prizes each year and do several dozen portraits, but I'm not deluding myself.

"You will know when I am finished," I said.

"That's not what I was saying," Sophie protested. "My point was that because you've got a finite number of pictures left, you shouldn't be wasting time writing articles."

"Need that finite number change?" I asked.

Sophie looked irritated.

"I'm not a juke box. You don't just put your money in a slot and get a portrait. Mind you, one day you might."

"Oh, be serious!" she said, exasperated. "I just don't want you wasting your time and talent."

I finished my coffee, folded my napkin and put it on the table.

"I have already resolved that my last portrait will be another one of you. You probably won't want to pose for it, but I can paint you in my sleep. This will be one final, full-size portrait and I have already cleared a wall for it in my set."

I walked with Sophie to the car in silence. I'd drunk sixty percent of the wine, so she was fine to drive.

Before she closed the door, she looked at me.

"How do you think I'll feel if I see you doing that painting?"

Her voice was a whisper; the thought had upset her more than I thought.

"Do I not deserve a retirement?"

She gave me one last look of exasperation, closed the door and drove off.

☙

Back in my room I reviewed what I had drawn that day. Of the fourteen sketches, two would develop well and I could tick them off the list.

This was one of those funny jobs where the client wanted to see things immediately as if a painter were a Polaroid camera. Marissa had unobtrusively looked over my shoulder a few times during the day, but didn't interfere and said nothing.

The reality is that the drawings would be inked – or copied – offsite and coloured in the studio. I had explained this, but knew not to expect things to stick in Marissa's mind. In fairness, she was busy, and I was just one more thing to manage.

I made it to the site by eight-thirty the next morning, well in advance of the team. I used the uninterrupted time to set up and to do some measurements of the building, pacing out the inside and outside and estimating the height of the remaining walls and dimensions of the windows.

The plan to excavate to see if there was a floor seemed to be a good one. The door into the building had been hacked about when it was converted into a barn or an enclosure, so the doorway was higher than normal doors. There were dressed stones used as corbels with bricks forming the arch and infill. Had I been asked, I would have guessed there would be a cobblestone floor, though it may have been laid above stone or brick.

I set up my chair in the corner and had been drawing for about ten minutes when Max Hillyard came in.

"Good morning, Sir Nigel," he said, tapping his floppy hat. "Early starts are good."

"I wanted to do a few things before the site got busy," I said. "Tell me where you'd like me to be – or not be – and I'll move."

He began moving behind me to steal a look at my sketch.

"May I?"

"Of course," I said. "I was still speculating on the original use of this building."

Max laughed.

"I've been doing that since I first saw it," he said.

"I am surprised by one thing," I ventured.

"And that is?"

"Why there's not more stone in this building. If my guess about its age is right, there should have been a fair bit of stone from the priory and Bickering Hall lying about," I said. "If the window at Bickering Place is anything to go by, wouldn't you expect to see more pre-Tudor brick and stone?"

He walked around to face me.

"Marissa said you knew what you were talking about," he said.

It was my turn to laugh.

"I don't know what made her said that," I said. "We had relatively few conversations about anything substantial that wasn't about the portrait."

Max thought for a moment.

"You know, she didn't like it at first," I continued.

Max shook his head.

"She was just surprised," Max replied.

"She told you about it?"

"Oh, yes," he said, rather sadly. "She tells me everything, but it never gets further than that. Anyway, the portrait. You caught her really well, but you also caught what she could be – and *wants* to be."

I'd been drawing while he spoke and continued to do so although I wanted to stop and think about what he had said.

"Good morning, darling," Sophie called from the entrance.

"That's what I'd like to hear," Max said, with a laugh. "You should be all right where you are this morning."

"Was I interrupting?" Sophie asked, when she came closer.

"Not really. Max was beginning to give me a bit of insight into Marissa. I expect he'll tell me more later."

"Maybe. Just remember, you're here to work."

Chapter Seven

Wednesday

We all worked hard that morning. Max and Marissa organised the diggers, the sifters and the wheelbarrows. They had chosen a line reaching from a front corner of the space to the middle of the room for the first trench. After some discussion, they also agreed to dig along the front wall from the corner and across about a third of the opening to see if there were a stone threshold or foundation.

I didn't know what, if anything, had gone on behind the scenes, but the two of them worked closely and well, agreeing with each other's approach and instructions. They had been taught by the same people, so on one level, it made sense, and they appeared to accept the other's decisions easily.

I was intrigued because Marissa hadn't struck me as being able to separate the personal from the professional.

They moved off to start the process while I continued to draw. I made very quick sketches of people snapping coloured chalk lines, and driving stakes in the ground and spraying them with bright orange paint.

Tools were handed out and, after a few minutes, the work settled into a rhythm. It was fascinating to watch, and I took the time to make some sketches of the various jobs being carried out: digging, sifting, sifting again and taking the dirt off by wheelbarrow. As I got to know everyone's names, I added them to the sketches.

While the teams took a quick break, Sophie came over to see how I'd been getting on.

"Any interesting finds?" I asked.

"What you'd expect: horseshoe nails, screws, buttons, bits of wire and a rusted horseshoe. There were a few bits that we guessed were fasteners and pieces of buckles from bridles, but very little, really," she said.

"I suppose that if this were used as a barn, the floor would have to be clear of anything that could harm the animals."

The woman who had been doing the first screening with Sophie came up. Sophie introduced us. Doris was the wife of one of the farm workers.

"Come on Sophie," she said. "They're digging again; we don't want to miss any exciting nuts and bolts."

I stood and walked around. I'd been sitting for nearly an hour and a half and was beginning to feel the chill. It was too crowded and busy inside the building, so I went to see how the digging around the foundation was going. The trench already reached the prescribed distance across the threshold, but had only gone down about six inches.

Outside, the walls were now bare of vines and brambles. The land behind the building was only about ten feet from farmland so was kept cut back but not mown. The grass and undergrowth had been trampled and the ground near the wall had been cleared to about eighteen inches from the building. Digging looked about to begin.

I fetched my chair and materials and, after checking with the team, placed myself where I'd be out of the way.

Looking at the windows from this side confirmed my impression that this had been a chapel. Had it been a few centuries younger, I might have guessed a school house. Supporting this theory was the absence of any evidence of any inside walls in the building, but then again, there would have been stalls and pens, and there was no sign of them, either.

After a few sketches, I began a careful drawing of the building, trying to achieve near brick-by-brick authenticity. There would be photographs, and I was not there to make architectural drawings.

The team, which seemed to be led by a young full-bearded man called Harry, began to open a three-foot trench along the centre of the wall. I snapped a quick picture with my phone as he was an interesting character essentially working on his own.

Although I continued to draw steadily for about an hour and a half, my concentration was interrupted by thoughts of what Sophie wanted to show me and the seed of doubt she had planted in my ability to write the introduction for Powell.

The sound of the digging was oddly calming and made concentration easier. Wheelbarrows with sifted earth were dumped not far from where I was sitting, and a gentle chatter drifted over the wall, punctuated with occasional laughter, or a sudden shouted instruction.

The motley team had gelled and was working smoothly under Max's quiet coaching.

I wrapped up my pencils, rubber, ruler and bits, and wander up to Harry to see his progress.

He stopped to look up at me.

"How are you getting on?" I asked.

He stood back so I could see. He'd opened a three foot trench against the building that had exposed five courses of bricks.

"It's amazing how the ground level rises over time," he said. "I think it must be getting close to a foundation. The trouble is that to go much deeper, I'll need a longer and wider trench. I'll have to talk Max into that over lunch."

When Marissa blew the whistle for lunch, Sophie came up to me and helped carry my pads and notebooks.

"Are the young people running rings around you?" I asked.

"Shall I just throw these into the ditch here, or do you want me to chuck them out the window of the car?"

I looked at her.

"Is *that* how you ask me for a ride?"

We laughed.

In the car, I asked her if she'd found anything interesting while sifting earth.

"More of the same. Max thinks the use might have changed because of the number of nails," she said. "He said it looked like it had moved from animals, to a workshop and then storage, but what it was used for first, he didn't say.

"Still, I found a 1900 penny and a 1920s threepenny bit," she added with satisfaction.

"The half-silver one?"

"Yes."

"No earlier coins?"

"Not yet."

৪০

April had prepared lunch for a ravenous team. A thick beef stew, mashed potatoes or rice, carrots, mushrooms and plenty of bread. Beer and wine were available along with strong coffee and tea.

I was content to let the real workers go in first after washing and removing our boots, but they treated me as old and Sophie as a celebrity and let us enter the kitchen as soon as we were clean enough.

We took our meal to the conservatory where extra chairs and tables had been set out and joined several others.

Rather than a group discussion, several private ones were going on, so Sophie and I had a chance to talk about other things.

"You succeeded in making me worry about writing for Powell," I opened. "That kept me awake last night and distracted me this morning."

She regarded me suspiciously, aware that I had overstated things.

"It will be fine," she said, "just leave plenty of time to do it. See if you can get most of a draft done by the time my run ends."

"Do I research it, or just write it?" I asked.

"I think a few scholarly observations that can be supported are in order. You owe it to David to do that much."

"Did they hit a floor anywhere this morning?"

Sophie shook her head. I told her that Harry had dug down five courses without reaching any foundation stones.

"It's not Harry," Sophie corrected. "His name is Derek."

"I'm sure I heard him called Harry," I protested.

Sophie laughed.

"No, they call him Hairy," she giggled. "It's okay, he doesn't mind."

"Does he work on the farm?"

Sophie shook her head.

"He's a former colleague of Marissa's from the estate agency. She's trying to tempt him to manage the farm."

"Potential boyfriend?"

"I don't think so."

"She's very good at using people," I said, softly.

Sophie giggled again and said, "Shh!"

We had finished our meal.

"Are you going to show me what you've been tantalising me about?"

She nodded and put her napkin down. We took our dishes into the kitchen then headed to the stairs leading to Sophie's room. I stopped for a second to look at the portrait to ensure it was straight.

"Did I show you where I signed it?" I asked Sophie. "Here in the pattern of the oriental rug."

She leaned forward to take a closer look, then started up the stairs.

My foot was on the first step when I felt a hand on my arm.

"I don't know what you two were planning to do up there, but I want to talk to Sir Nigel before we head back to the site."

It was Marissa.

I glanced at Sophie before turning to Marissa. For the first time in all my encounters with Marissa, Sophie looked put out.

"Sophie won't mind if I borrow you," she said, putting her arm around me. "I want to see how you are getting on before we have to go back to the site."

I explained that my things were in the car.

"I'll wait in the conservatory while you fetch them."

Chapter Eight

Wednesday

By the time I returned to the conservatory with the sketch books, Marissa had cleared the room and was seated on the sofa. I thought she looked tired, but satisfied and thought she had every right to be both.

I selected one of the sketch books and sat next to her. I showed her the list of positions I had made based on her briefing and how the sketches were numbered to indicate which. Next, I showed her the smaller character sketches, and then the larger, more developed ones.

She looked with more seriousness than I expected.

"I like the way you've shown all the different jobs," she said, turning the pages.

"There are three more scenes to do. I'd like to have one sketch of everyone. There are only about four more people to catch – at least of the ones I've seen."

She thought for a moment, flipping pages back and forth.

"I'd like to buy all of these," she said. "I can give everyone a picture of themselves. These are fine the way they are."

She then considered the larger pictures that were on the list.

"I'll develop water colours of all of these," I said.

"Will you colour these, or draw new ones?"

"Some and some. Some might need the composition changed a little, at least one needs to be done again because of damage to the paper. That's the risk of *plein air* work."

She looked closely at one of them.

"What I love about the sketches is their spontaneity. Try not to lose that in the ones you have to re-do."

She looked at her watch. It was time to go, but she didn't budge.

"How many of the set pictures have you done?"

"Five of twelve, in very basic outlines."

She nodded.

"That's good. You have three more days, so completing them and the little personal pictures shouldn't be a problem?"

"No. I think I'm good for time. They'll be completed in the studio."

Her formality broke, and she took my arm, giving a little squeeze.

"There's no reason why you couldn't stay longer."

෩

When I went to the car, I found Sophie already in it, waiting. She said nothing as I got in, and nothing as we drove to the site. It was the silence of a married couple or lovers. Since we were neither, I didn't have to put up with it, so I joined the silence.

After I parked and she got out, I just said, "Have a good afternoon," and she went off to get her sieve. Not a particularly sensitive move, I know, but all I had done was to meet with my employer.

I knew an idiotic argument could interrupt my concentration, but, of course, so would the adolescent silence.

Rather than go back to the place where I'd been working, I decided to move about the site and block in the rest of the "shots" that Marissa wanted. It would make a change from sitting still, and also help me understand and plan the work remaining.

While doing that, I was able to do two of the four remaining "character sketches" and also re-evaluate my personal conclusions about the building.

I had just stood up and was about to head to the car for my thermos flask when one of the diggers let out a cry.

"Floor! I've got a floor!"

We all rushed over to the diagonal trench, where nearing the centre of the building, some brick and cobble could be seen.

Max stooped down and stared into the eighteen-inch trench, and nodded.

Marissa was next to him.

"This explains the quantity of nails we've been finding in the last few loads," he said.

We all looked at him waiting for an explanation.

"I think they're from a wooden floor that went over the stone and brick one," he said.

I glanced at Sophie. She still held her sieve and was listening closely to Max.

"Well done, everyone," Marissa said, loudly. "Let's see what else we can find."

We went back to work, but for the rest of the afternoon, people would pass by the trench to see how much more floor had been uncovered.

With an extra man in the diagonal trench, it was excavated down to floor level fairly quickly. Following a consultation with Marissa, Max then instructed the diggers to widen the trench by a foot so they could prepare for a larger team to get on with a full clearance.

This put pressure on the sifters, but Marissa told them that there would be more tomorrow. I could see Sophie continuing her steady rate, and not be bullied into working more quickly.

About five minutes before stopping time, Sophie had obviously spotted something in her sieve. She took it to Max and Marissa, and the three of them were huddled over whatever it was.

Marissa's involvement with the new find didn't stop her from blowing her whistle on time.

"Thank you everyone!" she called. "It's been a very successful day. The first round of drinks will be on me at the Coach and Horses."

A few cheered while others gave murmurs of appreciation. It took about twenty minutes for the tools to be brushed down and stowed. I needed two trips to the car to load my chair and bits and pieces.

The Coach and Horses was about five miles from the site, but only three from Horncastle, so I decided to go. It would be good to have a chance to talk to the people I'd been drawing. No doubt they wondered about the old duffer who just sat around all day playing with pencils.

It was early, so the pub was empty when the team descended. It became clear that there were several groups: those from the farm, those who knew Max, and those who knew Marissa from the estate agents. Added to those cliques were Sophie and me.

After getting my drink and a pint for a chap called Brian who had spoken to me briefly on both my days on the dig, Marissa clanged the 'Last Orders' bell. Max stood next to her.

"Well done, everyone and thank you," he began. "We have two things to celebrate this evening – "

The party, anticipating a romantic announcement, gave expressions from, "Ooooh!" and "Fwhoar!" to "About time!" and "Who finally said yes?" followed by applause.

I don't remember seeing Marissa blush. I had seen her turn puce with outrage (usually at her mother), but blush? I didn't think so. However, in the blushing stakes, it was Max who was the clear winner.

Marissa recovered first, waving at her friends to be quiet.

"At present, the things to celebrate are related to the dig," she said, with impressive command. "The first is that we found and uncovered the floor. Secondly, with about ten minutes to go, our celebrity digger discovered the first unexpected find of the dig."

I looked around for Sophie, as did the others, but she was not there.

"Max, why don't you tell us what it was – and do it quickly before everyone dies of thirst," Marissa teased.

Max held up a small sealed bag which had a label and identifiers written on it. He passed it to the person next to him whose name I didn't know.

"As you can see, it's a lead ball," he said. "We are lucky to have Rachel Rawding on the site, whose unexpected avocation is firearms. Rachel has identified this as a .38 projectile.

"When there has been time to examine it properly, we'll let you know what we've found out," Max concluded.

"Enjoy the evening," Marissa called.

I glanced at my watch, it was not yet six. Sophie had not turned up. Marissa's departure made me think that she, Sophie and April had arranged to do something, or just retreat from the crowd and enjoy the quiet of their house before their lodgers rolled in.

I turned to the bar to buy some nuts, biltong, or something.

"How's your work coming, Sir Nigel?"

The speaker was an attractive lady, about the same age as Marissa, with dark hair and darker eyes. Like the rest of us, she wore earth on her clothing and was without makeup. Her hair was pulled back tightly. I was held by her eyes, so did not immediately notice much else.

She held out a hand.

"I'm Rachel Rawding."

"You are one of the two people here I haven't drawn yet."

She looked surprised.

"I'm sorry, what are you drinking?"

"Just a lemonade, thank you," she said. "You're drawing everyone?"

"Just quick sketches."

I ordered her lemonade and a half Guinness to top up my pint.

"Which group do you belong to? Max's friends, Marissa's, the estate agency or the farm?"

Rachel laughed.

"You've got us all sorted," she replied, but there was the hint of an edge to her voice. "I fall into several of those camps. My husband knew Titus and April Gilliat, and I've known Marissa since primary school, though I was a year ahead of her.

"Consequently, I know people from the farm and around. This is a very small place, you know," she added with a smile.

"I'm sorry – "

"I know, bar chat," she laughed, easily now. "You did that painting of Marissa, didn't you. You're here with Ligeia Gordon, aren't you? What's she like?"

"Haven't you spoken to her?"

"Only to say hello to, or pass the pepper at lunch, though I expect I'll talk to her more since she found the lead ball."

"And you're the arms expert."

"Well, I know more than the others, but it should be looked at by someone who really knows."

"Would it be unusual to find a ball like that there?" I asked.

"Actually, it would," she said. "If the building was being used as a barn at the time, any slaughtering will have been done outside – not that animals were usually shot."

We finished our drinks. I could see Rachel wanted to talk to some friends, and I wanted some supper.

As I stepped back from the bar, she said:

"It will have to be confirmed, but I think that ball was shot through a rifled barrel. Given the age, that should limit the choice of weapon. See you tomorrow. I'll try to keep still enough to sketch."

Chapter Nine

Wednesday

It had just gone eight when I entered the dining room at the hotel. For a Wednesday, it was reasonably busy. A few tables away, there was a noisy birthday or hen night in progress, and dotted about were several businessmen on their own.

I was leafing through a magazine that didn't require much concentration as I drank a glass of Merlot and waited for my meal, in this case, *The Journal of the London Mathematical Society*. I hadn't kept up with my reading, so this was not the current issue. An article, "Hamiltonian circle actions on complete intersections," caught my eye and I didn't pay as much attention to my food as I should have.

I was so absorbed that I failed to notice Sophie approaching the table. I closed the magazine and stood up.

"May I join you?" she asked, with mock formality.

"I thought you'd gone back to have a quiet evening with April. Is something wrong?"

She took the seat opposite me and sat down.

"Is your coffee good?" she asked.

Anyone who didn't know her would think her insufferably rude, but it was just part of the way we communicated. She was of the generation when, at boarding school, you didn't ask someone to pass the salt, but you offered it to the person who was nearest it: "Would you like some salt?" "No, thank you. Would you?" "Yes, please."

I always thought that knowing this simple custom would help foreigners understand the British better than more lengthy explanations. The whole disposition of diplomacy is exemplified in that simple exchange.

I signalled the waiter and Sophie's wish was fulfilled.

"So, what brings you here?"

"Just another smirch on our reputations," she replied. "After our failed effort to escape to my bedroom at lunchtime, I explained to April and Marissa that there were a few pictures in the back of the cupboard under the eaves in my bedroom that I wanted you to see.

"Marissa had the grace to be embarrassed by stopping us and readily agreed to let me bring them to you here so you can consider them for a few days. They're in the car."

Sophie was in no rush to get back to April's and took her time drinking her coffee. When she finished, we went to the car park and retrieved three black bin-liners containing rectangular shapes ranging from about eight by ten inches to a formidable twenty-eight by thirty-two inches. I carried the large one from the bottom while Sophie carried the other two.

In the hotel lobby, I pushed the button for the lift.

"Prepare for another smirch."

Sophie giggled as she stepped in, and continued to giggle until the doors opened on the second floor.

"Just how delicate are these things?" I asked.

"April said that if they crumbled into splinters not to worry. She said that they hadn't been hung in at least two hundred years and no one was likely to in the next century."

"Don't over praise them," I said.

I cleared the table in my sitting room and Sophie carefully laid the sack with the smallest picture on it.

I went into the bedroom and returned with two pairs of latex gloves.

"We should have cotton, but these will be better than nothing."

We snapped them on and Sophie burst out laughing.

"Ready when you are, Doctor."

I don't think younger people imagine people our age giggling.

I opened the unsealed bag and withdrew a small panel with an oil portrait. I turned it so we could see it right-side up.

"Oh, my," I am told I said.

Before me was an unframed portrait of a lady on a wooden panel. It seemed to be from the Tudor period but there was little to identify it as British, French or Dutch. Part of the problem was that at some point, it had been in a fire and the paint had cracked into thousands of surprisingly regular pieces that cupped away from the panel and looked about to fall off, yet none had.

I went back to the bedroom to retrieve my magnifying glass. I hadn't brought my headset, but this would do. Sophie had taken the LED lamp from the desk and placed it over the portrait.

"What colour do you want?" she asked, as if selling ice cream.

"Start with the incandescent and then we can see if the other tones add anything," I said. "This is hardly scientific, but it's a start."

"Shouldn't we be wearing masks?" she asked, sitting back and taking off her gloves.

"Afraid you'll get the plague?" I asked. "I think there's little chance of that."

"No, to protect the picture, you wally!"

"We're not going to do more damage than the last five hundred years has done as long as we're sensible," I said.

"Did you look at the white of her bib?" I asked. "Part of it has yellowed, but other bits are still quite white. But, use the glass: what do you see?"

She examined the image closely.

"Is that discoloured varnish?"

"Yes. And – "

She stood up and put the glass down.

"Soot."

I nodded.

"Baked in. Unless it comes off with the varnish, it will be impossible to restore, but it should be seen," I said. The picture was very dirty, so once again, I left to fetch a watercolour mop brush used for washes. I hadn't used it this week, so it was dry.

Carefully, I began brushing dust from a small area around the figure's throat where a small pendant fell from a gold jewelled choker. I stared at it through the magnifying glass for nearly a minute, changing the angle of the lamp.

"Nigel?" Sophie prompted, in concern.

I stood up, then sat down in one of the chairs.

"Are you all right?"

I smiled.

"Yes, I'm fine. Just surprised," I said. "Here, have a look at the pendant. Tell me what you think it is."

Sophie bent over the picture and also fiddled with the lamp, then she, too, sat down.

"Is that what I think it is?" she asked, in a whisper.

"Let's check it under the other colour tones," I said.

Sophie switched it to a whiter tone and looked again before switching to the blue-white.

"It doesn't seem to make much difference," she said. "It's hard to make out; it's so dark."

"There appears to have been an attempt to hide it at some point by painting the pearl over it, but you can still see it," I said.

She handed me the glass and switched the tones as I looked.

"No," I agreed. "But, in spite of the dirt, discoloured varnish and *craquelure*, there's no doubt that it's a white boar."

Sophie's eyes widened.

I straightened up and looked at the whole portrait.

"Do you think Marissa will let me take it to London?"

Sophie gave her full laugh.

"Marissa will let you do *anything*."

❦

"Do you want to see the next one?"

She lifted the second bag onto the table. It was an unframed canvas of about twelve by eighteen inches.

I moved the lamp to give the best illumination. To me it looked like a not very good late eighteenth or early nineteenth century landscape. There was a pond with a duck or two, a nearly flat landscape, and a ruin so completely demolished that it was without any architectural interest. This painting was even more filthy than the portrait, probably because the amateur painter didn't know when to stop with the varnish. What was of some interest, and may offer a clue if the painter proved to be more competent than it now looked, was a fantastical sunset at the far left.

"I suppose this should be looked at in the event that it's a sketch by a known artist, but to me it's pretty uninteresting," I said. "If it's a view from around here, it may have some interest. It's painted from a hilltop and by an amateur with some ability."

"Careful, it's probably an early Constable or Turner," Sophie laughed. "We're just prejudiced against the Romantics. You should take it with you just to be sure."

I put it away and lifted the largest picture onto the table. Sophie helped me, holding the bag as I withdrew it.

"This is more interesting," I said, as I oriented it properly.

I remember myself as saying, "Oh, my!" again, but Sophie insists I said, "Good lord!"

It looked very much like a Renaissance floral painting, the sort seen in museums all over the world. I stood the picture up and moved to look at the back. It was on a strainer which accounted for the distortions in the canvas, but there were no markings on it at all. The dust and dirt made it hard to be sure, but didn't look like it had been relined.

I began going over it with the glass. Even through the dirt and varnish, I could see it was beautifully painted.

I am not an art historian, nor an expert on any sort of painting, but having seen and studied so many over forty years, a sense develops. Just as a concert goer can tell Beethoven from Brahms without any special musical knowledge, this painting was telling me it was English. I couldn't articulate why, or what the clues were, but that was the impression I had.

The second impression I had was that this painting shouldn't exist.

So engrossed with the picture was I that I didn't notice Sophie leaving the room and asked her a question only to find her not there.

I looked at my watch. It was nearly eleven-thirty. I figured she'd slipped out and gone back to Bickering Place. I wrote a few observations in my notebook, put the painting back in the bin-liner, and turned off the light and went into the bedroom.

I was startled to find Sophie on the second double bed in my room, still fully clothed, but sleeping peacefully.

There go our reputations.

Again.

Chapter Ten

Thursday

When I woke Thursday morning, Sophie was gone. I was going to have to think of a way of greeting her on the dig that stopped her from telling me what a selfish bore I am. However, Sophie surprised me, as she often did.

"I'm so sorry about last night," she said, as she greeted me when I parked the car at the site. "I was just so tired."

"You were working all day. I was just sitting around."

"I was hoping you'd understand."

We walked around the building, checking the state of Hairy's trench which now revealed a few inches of underdressed stone foundation.

Inside, Max was talking to the various diggers and to Marissa. I would have to find an opportune moment to ask her about taking her paintings to London.

"Are you going to tell her about the pendant?" Sophie asked.

"Why not? She might have a family story that explains it."

"Good point," she conceded. "Lunchtime will probably be the best time to catch her."

I agreed and went back to the car for the rest of the tools of my trade while Sophie put on her gloves and collected her sieve.

On the way to the car, I met Rachel Rawding heading into the building.

After greeting each other, she stopped.

"Where will you be working today?" I asked. "You're the last one I need to draw."

She laughed.

"Max wants the trench at the entrance lengthened. Now that there's a floor, there's a good chance of finding a threshold stone. Several of us will be working on that," she said. "They're going to put something across the existing trench for people to walk over."

"I'll see you there."

Finding a place to sit in the front part of the building was becoming difficult as the excavations of the floor extended. The route for the wheelbarrows needed to be kept unobstructed, and the presence of a septuagenarian in a director's chair not seeming to be doing much of anything was incongruous.

To me, at least.

The people on the team were very kind, and having had a chance to speak to almost all of them, I hoped went someway to justifying my existence. Last night at the pub had helped a lot, and no one seemed reluctant to say good morning.

At nine o'clock, Marissa blew her whistle and Max outlined the plans for the day. He noted that things had settled into a comfortable and steady rhythm which he hoped could keep going.

I had placed my chair as far from the entrance as I could without being in the way or having my view obstructed. I was against the wall about halfway into the building and looking towards the entrance. Not only did it enable me to sketch the diggers at the threshold but the wider view made for a dramatic scene.

I looked over to Sophie who had swapped sifting duties with Doris; Sophie would be pleased to find more than nails and buttons.

I began by drawing the larger scene at the entrance. Even with only a few lines on the paper, I could see the final watercolour. Sometimes things worked this way.

"MAX!" I heard Sophie cry. Given her RADA voice, I expect that whole part of Lincolnshire heard her.

I looked up to see if she had been hurt, but she was holding a find high in the air and waving. Though others looked to see what she had, she showed no one until she placed it into Max's hand. Marissa had joined him as soon as he took the object from Max.

"*Rachel!*" Max called, looking up.

Rachel moved quickly to them, and I turned my chair and reached for my phone. Before my view was obstructed by others, I managed to take a satisfying picture of Max, Marissa, Rachel and Sophie looking at the find.

After a minute, Marissa told everyone to get back to work and she, Max and Rachel left the building to talk about what had been found.

I continued my work on "Diggers at the Threshold" until eleven when we broke for coffee.

Sophie came over to me while I was making things safe.

"So what did you find – or is that classified?"

She laughed.

"It was very rusty and clogged with dirt, but it was the chamber for an old revolver," she said.

"Ah, and did it fire the ball you found yesterday?" I asked facetiously.

"Almost certainly," came Rachel's voice from behind me. "Good morning, Sir Nigel."

"Rachel, you haven't met Sophie properly, have you: Sophie Gregg, Rachel Rawding."

"Dame Ligeia," Rachel responded, extending her hand. "I saw you in *The Philadelphia Story* in Manchester, and I laughed all the way through *A Flea in Her Ear* a few years ago. Sorry, I don't mean to fawn."

"I'm glad you enjoyed them, and please call me Sophie." Then she dropped her voice, "And call *him* Nigel. I don't want him to get ideas above his station."

This caused Rachel to laugh, but she recovered herself quickly to return to the subject.

"I'd like to look at this chamber with an expert when it's cleaner, but I think it stands a very good chance of having held the ball Sophie found yesterday," she explained.

"If it's what I think it is, it came from a Colt 1851 Navy pistol – Navy was the model but it was used by the army, too," she explained.

"Colt's American, isn't it?" Sophie asked.

Rachel nodded.

"They had a factory in London, too. This was known as the 'London model.' It was widely used here, too."

"Would it have fallen apart like that?"

Rachel shrugged.

"That's one of the things we need to find out. Another is, where's the rest of it?"

We walked slowly to join other diggers for a chat.

"You might ask Max to see the other finds," Sophie suggested. "There may be a few unidentified things that you could make sense of."

There was a new buzz among the team with some amusing speculations. One of the diggers was trying to convince a few of his friends that the building could have been used as a shooting range for Dad's Army. No one immediately appreciated that WWII was in the wrong century for cap and ball firearms. There was a burst of laughter and ribaldry when the bluff was called.

"Marissa and Max must be very pleased with the way things are going," Sophie said.

"Finding a few things has lifted the burden," Rachel said. "There's a lot left to do, and only two weeks to finish."

"We'll be gone by the weekend," Sophie said. "I've got rehearsals coming up, but I expect Nigel will be coming back to deliver the pictures and see how things turned out."

Rachel was interrupted by Max, and Sophie and I moved away from the crowd, back towards where we were working.

"Find anything interesting this morning?" I asked her.

"A few large nails. A coach bolt," she said. "My screen is very coarse, but Doris didn't find much more."

Sophie regarded me for a moment.

"You seemed to know Rachel," she said, trying not to sound jealous.

I recognised the tone. I'd heard it many times in the past decade. Sometimes, I could tease her about it. Sophie took none of Marissa's flirtations seriously, but other times, I could tell that she perceived a threat from other women, especially sitters with whom I spent a lot of time.

At some level, Sophie knew that I had never fully got over the death of my young wife, Vera, many decades ago. She also knew that her own, shall we say, *limitations*, prevented her from altering our status quo, but I think she genuinely feared that I would disappear from her life.

"We talked last night at the pub," I said. "I wanted to find out where her interest in firearms came from, but wasn't able to."

"And were you sizing her up as a subject?"

I laughed, even though I had done so.

"She's attractive and interesting looking – "

"She's bloody beautiful – if in a little different way," Sophie said, louder than she intended.

The warning lights were flashing.

"Perhaps I should paint her as Lara Croft, or Xena, Warrior Princess."

"You're showing your age," Sophie said.

Another sign I was on dangerous ground.

"Who then?"

"Oh, I don't know. The Scarlet Witch? Morgan Le Fay?"

I considered this.

"Aren't they older than the ones I said?"

"Oh, Nigel," she sighed. "I do try to take you out. It would help if you had a television or went to the cinema. They're from *The Avengers*."

99

"What, Purdy, Tara King and Emma Peel?" I asked, still puzzled. "Now, Cathy Gale, *that* would be going back."

Maybe she realised that Rachel would be less of a threat than she feared, because she gave me one of her tolerant smiles.

ꙮ

When lunchtime finally rolled around, I was chilly and starving. Work was progressing. Hairy's trench had now exposed a foundation about halfway along the wall, and the threshold stone was just starting to come into view. There didn't seem to have been any remarkable finds, though Marissa and Max were called over a few times to see things that the sifters had found.

Sophie did a preliminary clean up before getting into the car with me.

"I still feel very embarrassed about last night," she said, when she'd slammed the door. "All of a sudden, I couldn't keep my eyes open."

"Your secret is safe with me," I said. "Did anyone see your walk of shame?"

"No, I went down the stairs, and they come out around the corner from the lift, so I could watch the desk," she said. "When the clerk went into the office for something, I slipped out. I'm probably on the CCD cameras, but no one is going to look unless there's been some incident."

I laughed.

"It's a wonder that the paparazzi haven't tracked you up here," I said.

"Little chance of that anymore," she replied, almost sadly.

Once we'd cleaned up at Bickering Place and went into the house, all I could think of was the thick soup I could smell.

Sophie and I carried our plates and mugs into the main front room where there was a large ancient table with wooden and folding metal chairs all around it. Others were already there and we ended up sitting opposite each other, with Rachel sitting next to Sophie.

"This is exciting," Rachel said. "Is it all right if I tell my friends that I had lunch with Ligeia Gordon?"

She asked it quietly because almost no one had recognised her in worn jeans, an old jumper and woolly hat.

I had to hide my big smile from Sophie who was actually embarrassed by the question.

"I won't if you don't want me to," Rachel said.

She gave me a quick look and I got a fleeting impression that she was teasing Sophie, but Sophie hadn't caught on. I thought some bomb-disposal work was in order.

"Did you have a chance to check the finds for anything related to the ball and chamber?" I asked Rachel.

She turned from Sophie with a big smile.

"I picked through the rusty bits and found two pieces that I am pretty sure went with the revolver," she said, enthusiastically.

"Could you identify them?" Sophie asked, relieved that the attention was off her.

"I think I found two pieces of the loading mechanism," she said. "With a cap and ball pistol, powder, ball and wadding need to be loaded into each chamber from the front.

"Underneath the barrel is a long thin metal rod that when pulled acts as a lever to drive the loading plunger into the chamber and ram the powder and ball home so it can be ignited and get the full power of the blast," she explained. "It looks clunky today, but was very advanced in the time before cartridges were introduced.

"I think I found the lever and the plunger."

Sophie nodded, taking in the explanation.

"How were those two pieces held together?" she asked.

"With screws," Rachel said. "There were a lot of rusty blobs in the finds, so they might be there."

"There *were* a lot of rusty blobs like that!" Sophie said laughing. "I don't know if they can ever be identified."

"I should think so," Rachel said. "They just need to be soaked for a few weeks in something to dissolve the rust."

"Why would those pieces be detached?" I asked. "A gun that's buried or just on the ground isn't going to unscrew itself."

"Now, that is a mystery," she replied, with a mischievous grin. "The pieces aren't damaged, so it wasn't kicked apart my sheep, goats, cows and pigs – though a hundred years of animal urine wouldn't be particularly good for it."

"How recently were animals kept there?" I asked.

Rachel shrugged.

Sophie looked at her watch.

"We should start making a move."

"Ah!" I exclaimed. "I need to ask Marissa about the pictures before she gets distracted."

Chapter Eleven

Thursday

As Sophie had predicted, Marissa was agreeable to the paintings being taken to London for a preliminary examination. She had known them all her life and never knew them to be hung.

"It was just junk that lived in the house," she said. "Because they were always there, no one felt they owned them, and so no one did anything about them."

I took the opportunity to show her the new drawings that she hadn't seen.

"The one of the doorway excavations is wonderful!" she exclaimed. "You know, that would make a fabulous oil painting – an echo of those nineteenth century Romantic scenes."

Marissa's "A" level in Art apparently had a lasting impact.

"When your watercolours and sketches are done and we all have a little more time, we'll talk more," she said, but all I could think about was getting back to London to show the paintings to a few people.

But who?

Driving back to the site, I asked Sophie.

"You could start with David Powell," she suggested. "It might be a good idea for a few discreet people before showing to your Royal Academy friends."

There was much wisdom in this. Showing people who would be apt to talk could do more harm than good. In all likelihood, these paintings deserved to be in the closet, and rumours of something sensational could get out of hand quickly.

Powell *would* be a good first stop. While not in the business of authentication, his opinion would mean that taking the paintings further would not waste the time of those who looked at them.

Next, I thought of Helena Stirakis, a conservator at the Courtauld Institute. I knew her from general art circles. More recently, I knew her from *The Storm on the Sea of Galilee* fiasco. Professionally, she was hard as nails and pulled no punches. Socially, she was charming and entertaining company. Dinner at the Savoy might buy her unofficial opinion.

That train of thought led me to James Beech, retired member of Scotland Yard's now-disbanded Art and Antiquities Unit. He lived in London and might be tempted to visit my studio on the promise of a good lunch – bringing down the average hospitality cost for all the opinions. Beech wasn't your usual art expert, but he had an uncanny instinct for uncovering fakes. He had shown dozens of experts and connoisseurs to be wrong. His findings had uncovered forgeries, conspiracies to fraud, tax evasion and money laundering. Museums and galleries welcomed him with dread as he could nearly single-handedly turn a fifty million pound thing of beauty into a worthless, loathsome thing. Though his job was catching criminals, he could turn an art collection into a patch of scorched earth.

Marissa had okayed "reasonable expenses" provided I didn't commission any work without getting her approval in advance. I thought I could get three good opinions for five hundred pounds worth of food and drink. I'd throw in the charm needed to do it for free.

෯

It had been a productive afternoon. While the morning had been largely occupied with the Diggers at the Threshold – which was not on my list of pictures to do – I had drawn another of the required pictures by three o'clock and had begun work on the final one.

The weather had been good and the afternoon sun shone brightly through one of the windows that had been unblocked.

At around quarter to four, Sophie let out her best theatrical scream then shouted for Max.

Everyone froze. Doris, who was working next to her, dropped her sieve. People began moving toward Sophie, but Marissa and Max were there in an instant.

I saw Sophie hold up her screen for them to see.

"Please clear the site!" Max shouted. "Take all your tools and equipment and clear the site."

Marissa checked her watch.

"You may go home," she called. "Thank you for another great day's work! Max or I will call you tonight and let you know about working tomorrow."

People looked puzzled, but Marissa was already on her mobile phone calling someone.

Sophie demurely handed her screen to Max and came to me.

"Are you all right?" I asked, giving her a quick hug. "What happened?"

She helped me put my things in the car, but said nothing.

"Let's go to the hotel," she said, quietly.

"You don't have April's car today?"

"I came with Marissa," she said. "I'm afraid you'll have to drive me back."

We were nearly at the hotel when Sophie began to talk.

She began by giving a short laugh.

"I found part of a human jaw bone," she said. "I was pretty sure what it was when I loaded my screen, but when I saw the teeth, there was no doubt. I've handled enough skeletons on stage and in films to recognise them pretty quickly."

"That must have been a shock," was all I could think of saying.

"That's the curious part, and why I needed to think," she said. "I looked at it and thought, 'Oh, a human jaw bone.' It took a few seconds to realise how significant this was, and that's when I screamed and called Max."

She gave another uneasy laugh.

"I screamed, not because I was startled or frightened, but because I was trying to decide whether to call Max or Marissa," she laughed again. "As soon as he asked everyone to leave, I knew that it would close the site."

"The place will probably be crawling with police."

I parked in the hotel lot.

"What do you want to do?" I asked her.

"I can't do much dressed like this," she said, "but I would like a shower."

"Then we can find someplace to eat without a dress code."

☙

Sophie was back to normal after her shower.

"It's early, but I'm hungry," she said.

"Anything in particular?"

"Dressed like this, I can't be too fussy, can I?"

Not far from the hotel, we found a Chinese restaurant that looked like it might let her in. The steaming tea placed on the table within seconds of sitting down was welcome.

"This week has been a bit different than London life," I said, and Sophie giggled.

I found several of my favourites on the menu and was torn between a Szechuan beef or a chicken subgum. Sophie was a sucker for any sort of fried rice as long as there was a lot of it.

She knew and liked food, but had only a passing interest in it. Something had to be pretty bad for her to criticise it. Her appetite always surprised me, but she never seemed to put on any weight. I knew she'd suffered from anorexia when she was thirty ("I was a late developer," she joked, darkly), and I wondered if that was part of it.

We ordered, and while we talked about the excavation, we didn't mention the bone or what it might mean. We'd go there when we had to.

"I'm sorry if I was snippy about Rachel," she said, and reached over to touch my hand. "She's only about forty."

Conversations like this cropped up from time to time, but I knew that whatever Sophie's heart wanted, her head prevented any action. I'd reconciled myself to it, and took Sophie's occasional displays of possessiveness simply as indications that at least she could feel something.

"I asked April about her," she said. "It's very sad."

Sophie was interrupted by the arrival of additional cutlery and two dish warmers, which had to be lit.

"She got a good degree and was teaching at Lincoln Minster School. She'd been there for nearly ten years when she fell in love and married a policeman with a promising future.

"After they were married and were settling into a rented cottage just up the road in Bardney, her husband was seconded to Scotland Yard. She continued teaching, and he came back on weekends," Sophie related. "April said it was very tough on them, but they knew it was short-term and he'd advance in the Lincolnshire force.

"Not long before he was due to return, he was killed in some operation," she said. "It made a lot of news at the time and several other officers were injured. Rachel was given an indefinite leave of absence – which may still be in force – "

Our meals arrived and we switched topic and pondered the future of the dig.

"The police are going to want to find the rest of the skeleton," Sophie said. "Marissa may get her site cleared down to the floor, but Max will be disappointed by the less than archaeological methods."

My Szechuan beef was excellent and Sophie seemed pleased with her prawn fried rice. We also had some side dishes whose names I have forgotten, but the vegetables were fresh and *al dente*. Pots of tea arrived on a regular basis.

"If the police are looking for more bones, they'll be fairly careful," I said. "The trick will be to separate any more revolver parts from the other rusted iron, but if they think it's a murder weapon, they might be careful."

Sophie drank some tea.

"Do you think everyone will be sent home?"

"We shall see," I said. "I'm ready to go home. I've got the sketches I need and I want to look at those paintings properly."

I told Sophie about my thoughts of other people to consult. She had heard about them from me, but hadn't met any of them. While I thought she might enjoy meeting David and Madeline Powell, I saw no point in introducing her to the others. Helena Stirakis would have caused more than the ripples that Rachel Rawding had.

We finished our meal and went back to the hotel. We didn't go in but got into my car, and I drove her back to Bickering Place.

Sophie was quiet on the way, but I put it down to the good meal and being tired.

The car crunched on the gravel sweep and I stopped to let her out.

"Why don't you come in?" she suggested. "You can find out what's happening."

She tapped the knocker and April answered quickly.

"Come in, Marissa and Max are just calling all the workers on the dig," she said. "It's a bit of a setback but rather exciting."

She beetled off into the kitchen.

Max and Marissa were on their phones in the main room explaining the situation. Marissa looked up, smiled waved to me, and quickly ended her call.

"Good, I can tell you in person," she said, coming up to me. "I fear we're thwarted until the police have finished with the site. At least the whole area will be excavated and sifted."

She looked and sounded tired. Max continued to make calls.

"Come into the kitchen," Marissa said, and we followed her.

We sat at the table.

"As expected, the police have secured the site. They've erected large tents so the excavations can be done out of site and in any weather."

"They started digging today, did they?" I asked, glancing at my watch.

"No, they took the jawbone and closed our operation officially," she replied. "I'm pleased to say that they were very satisfied with the way Max and I stopped looking ourselves and had the sense to recognise immediately that it was a possible crime scene."

Marissa's manner was more grown up than I'd ever seen it. At thirty-eight, she should be grown up, but this setback and her fatigue seem to deflate her more gregarious nature.

"So, you're shutting it down," Sophie said.

"We have to," she said. "With luck, when the police finish, we can get back to it."

I looked at Sophie then at Marissa.

"There's no point in me hanging around," I said, standing up. "I have all the drawings I need and I can work on them properly at my studio."

Marissa gave one of her big smiles and stood up, too.

"There's always a point of you hanging around here," she said, and I saw Sophie roll her eyes. "You are more than welcome to stay. We'll have lots of empty rooms by tomorrow night, but I understand."

I looked at Sophie.

"Will you come back Sunday as planned?"

"If that's all right with April and Marissa."

"I'll see you in London, then," I said, and blew her a kiss.

Marissa followed me to the door, then, taking my arm walked with me to the car.

"I'll see you here when you bring me my paintings," she said, as though she was talking about something else.

"Goodbye, Marissa."

Chapter Twelve

Friday

When I got back to the Captain John Smith Thursday night, it was just on the right side of being too late to call people, but I didn't think David Powell would mind anyway. If I could track him down. As it happened, he was in London for another two days and was intrigued by what I had to say.

"I've been given some old paintings by friends to have a look at and I'd value your opinion."

He gave me the usual, I'm not an expert spiel, and I told him that I'd prefer to waste his time rather than the real experts if he thought they were fakes or that I'd just embarrass myself.

I was confident that he'd accept for two reasons: first, he owed me a favour for writing his introduction, and secondly, I knew his curiosity would get the better of him. I told him he could bring Madeline if she wanted to come, and we'd go for a good lunch afterwards, so we arranged to meet the next day.

Despite the sudden curtailment of the dig, it had been a good experience, a break in the routine, and I had picked up an extra commission as well as the added amusement of Marissa's "closet paintings."

It was a very early start, but I managed to get to London and get rid of the car about half an hour before the Powells arrived.

I tidied the studio and just had time to pick up some croissants and a few pastries to have with coffee. Next, I set up three easels.

My main, most used, easel is an old wooden studio easel that I bought in a sale when I first set up as an artist. It must be a hundred years old. Like many of the period, it was on castors, but I later replaced them with modern casters with brakes, no doubt slashing its value as an antique. The second one was a wooden tripod easel with extendable legs, and the third was a collapsible one of tubular aluminium, ideal for painting on location. These last two were fitted with an arm that can grip the top of the canvas to change the angle of the plane of the canvas relative to the painter. (An "A" frame easel will hold a canvas securely, but it will lean slightly away from the artist. The arm can change that angle, moving the top of the canvas to the desired angle. This is particularly useful to painters who work sitting on a stool.)

I placed Marissa's paintings on the easels: the flower painting on the studio easel, and the smaller ones on the tripods. To create a bit of suspense and drama, and not to overwhelm Powell, I covered them with velvet drapes.

Once they were covered, I had a moment when I thought this was all a total waste of time; that Powell would think I was a fool and that he'd find someone else to write the introduction to his book.

A few minutes later, my buzzer rang and I told Powell to come up. I turned on the electric kettle then opened the door and went out to meet the lift.

Madeline stepped out first. She was younger than I remembered. I'd only seen her at press events and exhibition openings and only for long enough to exchange air kisses.

"This way," I said, directing them to my studio.

They entered and began looking around.

"I used to live here, then began using it exclusively as my studio when I moved to Albany."

"I'd love to see that," Madeline said.

"You are most welcome, but believe me, this is actually much more interesting," I said. "The light is good, and I have excellent artificial light, a kitchen, storage, and a bedroom where sitters can change, if necessary."

"The Southbank has changed a lot since you were first here," Powell said.

"Unrecognisable, but great fun. Good food, entertainment and safe," I said.

I made coffee and set the pastries on the dividing counter between the kitchen and studio proper.

We chatted generally, drank our coffee and Powell and I scoffed several pastries. We chatted about mutual friends, coming exhibitions, his book and other art world gossip.

Eventually, Madeline put a stop to it.

"Do you think we can do what we came here to do and go to lunch?"

The way she said it was funny, not impatient. It was curious that Powell and I spoke to each other the way we did because it seemed like we were older and better friends than we were. We were also close to the same age, though Madeline was considerably younger (and richer) which may have affected her priorities.

She walked towards the easels.

"This looks like a contest," she said, laughing.

"It is," I said. "The lady and the tiger."

"Nice concept," Powell said, approvingly. "A painted Medusa that kills the viewer."

I explained where the paintings had come from and why I wanted his impressions before showing them further.

"You're right about not wanting the tart world to get hold of this. Their gossip would have camera crews on your doorstep before the end of the day, and your carefully cultivated reticent image would be blown," he laughed.

I looked at Madeline.

"Has he always been like this?"

"Only since he met me," she replied, with only the hint of a smile.

For an instant, it was almost like looking in a mirror: the age difference between Powell and Madeline was even greater than that between Sophie and me.

I went to the first picture – the flower painting – and removed the covering. Even under my lights, the image looked dark and obscured. Colour did show through, hinting at something dazzling.

Powell and Madeline stared at it in silence, moving to see if a change in the angle would reveal anything. After a minute, Madeline sat down and drank more coffee, but Powell remained, silently staring, for nearly five minutes.

"This painting is trying to say something," he said, at length.

"What?"

"I don't know," he said, continuing to regard it closely. "Do you have magnifiers?"

I fetched my headset and gave it to him. He looked in silence for another two minutes.

"Do you know a really good restorer who could give this a thorough cleaning and keep his mouth shut?" he asked. "Independent? Discreet."

"Yes."

He moved his head around the picture and gave a short chuckle.

"Look, here, it's dirty, but can you see it?"

He pointed to an area in the lower right.

I retrieved my magnifying glass as Madeline came up to the canvas. I handed the glass to her.

"It's a ladybird," she said, with a smile.

"Have you got anyone in mind?" I asked.

He shook his head.

"Rachel Ruysch? Maria van Oosterwijck? Someone like that?

"Can I see the back?"

We eventually achieved that and inspected the canvas.

"It doesn't look like it's been relined, and the strainer looks right," he said. "A stretcher would be a good idea, I think. Ask your restorer."

We returned the picture to its previous position.

"I thought it looked like those seventeenth century Dutch paintings," I said.

"It does, but I think it's earlier," he said. "It's been a while since I looked, but check out Balthasar van Ast, but from what I see, this looks less fussy than your usual Dutch painter."

We stood back to give it a last look.

"What's next?" Powell asked.

I placed the drape over the flowers and removed the one from the portrait.

"She's had a bit of a rough night," he said, as soon as he saw it.

Under the lights and seeing the portrait with the freshness created by uncovering it, while the damage looked worse, the face looked enchanting.

Powell moved close and put on my headset again as Madeline came forward, too.

"She's lovely looking," she said. "What happened to her?"

"She's been in a fire," Powell said. "There's soot baked in and who knows what else on the surface."

He took off the magnifiers and stepped back.

"You've noticed what's curious," he asked me.

"I think so: with all the cupping and cracking, somehow the detail of the eyes and mouth are relatively undamaged."

"The choker and buttons, too," Madeline said.

Powell stood up straight and faced me as if waiting for a judgement.

"It could indicate that this is a forgery," I said. "That's why I'm having James Beech have a look."

Madeline looked puzzled. Before I could explain, Powell did.

"Scotland Yard expert."

"I didn't realise you knew him," I said.

"I don't," he said. "I've heard him speak a number of times, usually with other art historians. He'll tell you what you need to know in about thirty seconds."

We laughed.

"Now, David, did you catch what caught my eye?" I challenged.

He looked again but didn't seem to know where to focus.

"If it's real, how old do you think it is?"

"Mid-sixteenth century," he said, with some confidence.

"That's what I reckoned," I said. "Now, where do you think it was painted?"

He looked at it again.

"Could be anywhere: France, the Low Countries – "

He broke off and waved his hand at me.

"Give me the glass."

He'd found it.

"Bloody hell!" he exclaimed, after he'd looked. "Where did this come from?"

"I told you: an attic closet in a Tudor manor in Lincolnshire."

He laughed loudly and handed the glass to Madeline who wanted to see if she could detect what we were talking about.

We waited as she explored.

"Ah! The boar," she whispered.

"The boar."

"I think it's very wise that you are having Beech look at this next," Powell said. "It's nearly the perfect set-up."

Chapter Thirteen

Friday

Madeline said she was hungry, and Powell said he needed to digest the two things he'd just seen, so we left the viewing of the final painting and went to lunch.

We walked to one of the many wine bars that served decent food in Southwark and found a table by the window where we could watch the braver people who were eating outside.

I told them about the dig and how Sophie had found the pictures in the back of a cupboard in her room. I also relayed Marissa's observation that no one did anything with the old paintings because no one felt they owned them, and that no one really liked them well enough to hang.

Powell wanted to know about the house, but Madeline wanted to know more about the dig and how Dame Ligeia Gordon coped in wellies and mud. I filled them in but didn't mention the discovery of the jawbone.

David ordered a bottle of wine as we browsed the menu. Madeline chose quickly and put her menu down and gazed out the window.

When Powell and I had chosen, we looked at her.

"I was just thinking that young women are much better dressed now than when I was that age," she said, unprompted.

"Were you a Sloane Ranger?" I asked.

Madeline laughed.

"No, I was a bit of a geek," she said. "I was very much out as far as the Sloane crowd was concerned," she said. "The truth was that I wanted to be friends with some of the girls, but I had no interest in over-paying for fashion and accessories that would make me look even more frumpy."

"This from the lady who built a fashion accessories empire," Powell said, dryly.

"Do you remember the Sloanes?" I asked Powell. "Many are still around, but now they are the age they looked forty years ago."

"It was a bizarre fashion," Madeline said. "The fabrics were lovely but the designs were ghastly, and I was fated to be one who recognised it at the time.

"Look at the pictures of Diana before she was married," she continued. "She was twenty-two and looks middle-aged.

"The prices of mediocre accessories were based on the cachet of the brand. People have forgotten that the value of something is in its usefulness and quality, not in some 'perceived value' nonsense," she said.

She burst out laughing.

"I'm sorry," she said. "It's one of my hobby horses. I hope Ligeia Gordon wasn't a Sloane Ranger."

"No," I said. "She was spared that."

I looked at Powell who had said nothing.

"Don't look at me. I know nothing about fashion except when it was worn."

Our food arrived.

After a few minutes, Powell returned to the paintings.

"Do you have any idea who the lady is in the painting?"

"No. There's nothing on it to indicate who or what it is. As you saw, there are no labels or gallery marks."

"That would indicate that it was never sold which is why it's not known."

"I was going to take it to the Witt," I said. "At least, someone could say that it was a copy of the *Comtesse d'Ardeuil* or some such person."

Powell nodded.

"If Beech reckons it's pukka, will you fill me in on the known provenance. I'd love to research it," he said.

"David, you've got enough on with the book," Madeline protested.

"Come on, darling, you know you'd love all that time in London while I'm slaving away in the libraries," he replied.

"What have you been doing since you've been up?" I asked, not wanting him to comment on the flower painting and further irritate Madeline.

Madeline launched into projects at the flat, shopping trips, visits to friends and the theatre.

"It's a shame Ligeia Gordon isn't in anything at the moment. I'd love to see her," she said.

"So would I! See – another reason to spend more time here!" David exclaimed, amid laughter.

Our meals came and we managed to keep away from the subject of painting.

ဆ

Back at the studio, later than we had planned, before making more coffee to regain our critical decorum, I switched on the lights, uncovered the portrait again and gave Madeline and Powell the magnifying devices.

They stared at it until I handed them the coffee.

"I see three options," Powell said. "First, it's fake, and that's the end of the story. Secondly, it's real and was painted on the Continent and the woman is a refugee from the Tudors, but when and how it made its way back to England is a mystery. The third option is that this woman was a closet Plantagenet, and the picture remained a family secret."

I thought this was a good analysis and was along the lines I'd been thinking, but not fully formed or articulated. Nevertheless, a few wisps of thoughts arose and began to swirl in my mind.

"What's the final picture?" Madeline asked.

"I fear it's not as exciting as the first two, but once cleaned, may prove of interest."

I took the velvet cloth off and watched Powell's face.

The instant reaction was one that said it was a waste of time looking at it, but then he stepped forward and put on the headset.

"Do you know where this is?" Madeline asked.

"No. It could be anywhere," I said.

"Except it isn't," Powell corrected. "It is a very specific place. To find out where, the identifying clues need to be recognised for *what* they are, then we can work out *where* they are – or at least, were."

"You're being cryptic, David," Madeline said, in a carefully nuanced tone between chiding and teasing.

"Sorry," he said. "All I meant was that it is almost certain that this place is real. And while there are some attempts to create a sense of composition, things simply are where they are – "

"Or *were*," I put in.

"Exactly," David said, nodding to Madeline. "So, if – when – this filthy thing is cleaned – someone can identify a building or landscape feature, then the place can be identified."

He turned away from the painting.

"This is one of the dirtiest pictures I've ever seen."

Madeline gave him a sceptical look.

"I don't know, I've seen you look at some pretty dodgy pictures," she said, before giving him a big smile.

Powell smiled back instantly.

"Shh! I've got a reputation to keep, and Sir Nigel will report me to the pope."

While this exchange was going on, I removed the cover from the flower painting so he could consider all three.

"Here's another question," Powell said. "Were these part of the same collection or acquired separately?"

I laughed at this one.

"Darling, shall we buy that bunch of flowers, we've got a great closet we can put it in for two hundred years."

Madeline laughed, but Powell wasn't as amused, though he considered the remark.

"You're right," he said, after a moment. "It's a good argument for them having been in the same place."

"Or, returning from Europe when things were safer," I added, acknowledging his earlier point.

He motioned to me to flip the other painting around.

"Not a mark on any of them," I said. "No labels, no stencils, no pencil marks. I'll be sure they're looked at under UV lights, X-rayed, MRIed and CAT-scanned."

"There's certainly nothing that we can see," Powell agreed. "Not even evidence of glue where a label has been removed."

৪০

Powell and I then discussed his book and my introductory essay for about half an hour before they headed off to a fashion show that Madeline had been invited to. Powell was very funny about it, and Madeline played along with his pretended loathing of the prospect.

I could tell that Madeline wanted to meet Sophie, so I told them I'd be in touch when she got back from Lincolnshire. In fairness, I thought Sophie would like them very much.

It had been a good visit, and Powell had made a number of observations and suggestions that I wrote down as soon as they left. I could raise these with Beech at the next day's meeting. He could cull the field before I showed them to Dr Stirakis and embarrassed myself.

It's all too easy to get caught up with inappropriate ideas about unworthy paintings just because they were discovered in a cupboard of a house with Tudor origins, and I have to repeatedly tell myself that I'm a portrait painter, not an art historian.

I said as much to Sophie that evening when I called her.

My first question, of course, was, "Have they identified the body?" To which the answer was no, though she did have some news.

"Marissa and I drove to the site before breakfast. I think she wanted to beat Max there," she said. "The whole site was cordoned off with police tape and there were two cold constables there. Marissa had brought a thermos of coffee which they were pleased to have only if they went, one at a time, behind the building."

This made me laugh. I could imagine Marissa beguiling them into breaking the rules or being indiscreet.

"I expect she'd been to school with them," I said.

Sophie laughed.

"No. She was rather put out about that," she replied, still laughing. "They were both twelve years younger than her."

We both laughed at this for some time.

"I bet she just loved that," I said. "She probably wanted to take the coffee away from them."

"When we went back after breakfast, we found the detective inspector in charge who said that he'd recruited several of Marissa's team to continue digging, but that everything else would be handled by the police.

"I thought Marissa was going to kick up a fuss about it, but she had taken an interest in Detective Inspector Covell and simply said she'd check back later.

"And – darling, you'll love this – she took two steps away from him before turning to ask him for lunch at Bickering Place!"

I was about to say something, but Sophie continued.

"I think you've had a narrow escape!" she exclaimed.

After telling me a few more details about how the dig would have to be shelved for at least a week, I asked her her plans.

"April and Marissa have both asked me to stay to see how the skeleton saga turns out, but I told them I'd go back to London Sunday."

"Shall we go out or shall I cook?"

"Hmm," she pondered. "You can cook."

Chapter Fourteen

Saturday

I was looking forward to seeing James Beech. I hadn't seen him since I roped him into looking at some doubtful paintings that had come onto the market a few years before. Since then, I assumed he'd been living a quiet retirement and participating in the joys of London.

He had accepted my offer of lunch in exchange for looking at the pictures with an alacrity that suggested he was bored.

Like many of us, he had put on weight over the lockdown period, but still resembled a prop forward. Maintaining his level of fitness through a career in art fraud must have been difficult, but his work with the Art and Antiquities Unit occasionally led to a chase or a pugilistic encounter.

"I envy the way that you could sail through the retirement age without missing a brushstroke," he said, after we exchanged greetings and preliminary gossip over coffee.

Eventually, he stood and approached the three easels.

"Is there anything you want to tell me before I look at them?" he asked.

"I don't think so. I'll tell you what I can when you've had a chance to form an opinion."

He nodded.

"I had David Powell look at them yesterday for a general impression. I wanted you to look at them before I took them to Helena Stirakis in the event that you felt they were duds."

"Ah! The lovely Dr Stirakis," he said, and thought for a moment. "Are you on speaking terms with her after that business?"

"I think so," I said. "We've met at various events since, and she did agree to see me."

Beech stepped closer to the first painting.

"Okay, let's get started."

I removed the cloth and retreated back to the kitchen where I began making more coffee.

"May I turn it around?" Beech asked.

"Do what you need to. There are magnifiers on the shelf. Let me know if you want a hand."

Throughout his career, Beech had astounded art experts by latching on to some detail that would conclusively prove a painting to be genuine or a fake. Sometimes it was a tack in the stretcher, or discolouration that others would put down to age. He was also good at spotting fake labels, even if only a fragment remained.

His judgements were virtually immediate, but then he would look for a reason why he'd jumped to that conclusion. That often took time.

He had accumulated much art history and knowledge of paint and techniques along the way, but he acknowledged that what he had was a gift. Curators and experts had learned not to argue with it.

His experiences had given him a very jaundiced view of the art world, regarding it as little more than a legal vehicle for money laundering. Several museums banned him from entry after he retired from the police lest he call out too many pictures in their collections as fakes.

"May I see the next one?" he asked.

I removed the cover from the portrait.

His face lit up – I had only seen it do so on one other occasion when the x-ray of *The Rescue of Helen* confirmed his contention that it was by Titian, not "a follower of Titian."

I watched him as he looked at the portrait. I could tell immediately when he saw the muddled pendant. He put on my magnifiers and moved from side to side to see more thoroughly.

I turned the painting around for him so he could see the back of the panel. His face went back to being inscrutable and remained so even after I'd turned the picture back to facing him.

He showed no delight when I unveiled the last picture, but he studied it closely, front and back. Some areas he scrutinised, then stepped back and looked around for his coffee. In all, he'd spent about half an hour looking at the collection.

We sat down, and I waited for him to speak.

"You were going to tell me where these came from."

I gave a hollow laugh.

"When I say it out loud, it sounds like the perfect set up: they are from a 16th century house, overhauled in the Georgian style where they've been in a cupboard for two hundred years or more."

Beech laughed.

"Sounds like the opening to a murder mystery," he said.

It was hard not to tell him about the jawbone and all the police at the dig.

Beech thought for a moment.

"Well, it all fits. The pictures strike me as genuine. As to quality and meaning, I leave that to those who think they know better," he said. "The portrait is delightful. There is so much to say there – from being an early Tudor Plantagenet sympathiser to the fire in which she suffered so much damage."

"That was one thing that worried me," I said. "With all the cracking, is it realistic that her main features were essentially undamaged?"

"Good observation," he replied. "Yes, it's the first thing that would sound alarm bells, and most curators or assessors wouldn't get beyond that.

"The second alarm bell would be the lack of any discernible damage to the back of the picture – it's on a larch panel, by the way."

"But that doesn't worry you?"

"Not really. Everything else is solid and rings true."

"So those two things can be discounted?" I pressed.

"Ah, you want the two pint answer. Very well," he said. "We can assume that the painting was against the wall. Smoke rises, so it would have come up from below the picture, but the bottom of the frame would have been against the wall, so minimal smoke damage. There will be traces but to the naked eye, it's just four hundred years of dirt.

"Regarding the undamaged features, you just have to imagine the aftermath – this is what art historians and curators are surprisingly bad at."

Both Powell and Beech were good at creating likely scenarios when there was no hard evidence to go on.

"This would have been in a well-to-do household, he began. "When the ashes are cool enough, the family goes in to see what can be rescued. Many things can be identified, but are too badly burned to keep. Only those that are of some use are selected. This will not have been the only portrait in the house. This lady is young, a daughter. Surely, there will have been a painting of the owner, and probably his wife. Other children, perhaps, but they burned completely or were so disfigured that they weren't worth keeping – but this lady – whoever she is – this lady's face was relatively intact and recognisable, if damaged.

"Had her face been disfigured or the panel charred, no one would have bothered to save her," Beech said, with growing enthusiasm. "*The very reason she survived is the same reason why the curators are suspicious*."

I nodded.

"Natural selection in art," I ventured.

"Exactly! The *Winged Victory* and the *Venus de Milo* are beautiful enough without their head or arms, and that is why they have survived," Beech explained. "I've often thought that the attraction of the *Winged Victory* is that we all imagine the head on it. If the real one ever turned up, she'd inevitably be disappointing."

He looked at his watch.

"I'll tell you about the other two over lunch," he said cheerfully. "Where are we going?"

He was clearly in a good mood, and knowing that the three paintings were what they appeared to be, so was I.

"I thought we'd go to the King's Arms," I said, putting the drapes back on the paintings.

"Excellent. Harvey's."

CR

Not many people would know what beer was available at a randomly chosen pub, but Beech clearly had more than one talent. Newcomen Street wasn't far from my studio, so it only took a few minutes to get there. I'd reserved a table and after securing our drinks and perusing the menu, Beech resumed his critique.

"Unless there's more you want to know about the portrait, I suggest we move on to the flowers."

He took a swig from his pint and smiled in satisfaction.

"It's conceivable that they were from the same house," he began. "I think there is smoke on both sides of it, but it would have to be tested. As you can see, it was luckier than the portrait. It is about the same age. Again, I'd defer to the real experts, but I'd guess 1525 to 1575 for the portrait and 1550 to 1600 for the flowers."

This surprised me as the great flower paintings were 17th century, though there were some earlier.

"I don't know much about flowers, but I suspect the blossoms weren't chosen because they were in season," he added.

We ordered, having reached identical selections independently: whitebait and grilled rump-steak and chips.

"The landscape is much later – an early hint of Romanticism, but – I suspect – before 1800.

"Who are you getting to clean them? Someone discreet, I hope," he said, voicing my own reservations.

"There's a good team not far from my studio. Alicia Stephanini heads it."

"I don't know her," Beech said. "It will take time, but I suggest you have them all done before taking them to Lady Helena."

Helena had not been ennobled, but next to Beech's working class background, one could understand his comment.

"Are you going to have them restored?" Beech asked.

"I haven't the budget for that. Just a clean and a varnish," I said. "Though, I don't know if the portrait can be cleaned. I'll see if Alicia can tidy up the bits around the boar."

If Beech had other thoughts, he didn't share them, and our discussion moved on to the challenges of retirement.

I mentioned that I had seen Bill Warren and asked if he had heard from him.

"Not since before the plague," Beech said. "Once you sort out these antiques of yours, we should all meet for a meal – or better still, show up without warning on his doorstep in Sussex. Virginia would love that."

"Wouldn't she just!"

Chapter Fifteen

Saturday

Such was our meal and further pints that followed, that I took a taxi back to Albany. I had more notes to add to the ones I wrote after talking to Powell, and I wanted to call Alicia Stephanini. I hoped she'd answer her mobile.

I didn't know Alicia particularly well. We'd met at some gallery function, and I'd directed some business her way when she was getting established about five years before. With the lockdowns, I hoped she was still in business.

"I'm still at the studio," she said, when I called. "Oddly enough, I was able to stay open during the lockdowns because my space was considered manufacturing. I just had to contrive a separation between the workshop and a customer area. I was busier than ever."

I told her I had three pictures in need of help and asked when she might be able to do it.

"You are a lucky man today," she said. "And I am a lucky lady."

She told me that a big job that would involve her whole team would be a week late, leaving them with a gap in their schedules.

Restorers, like other craftsmen who carry out repairs, furniture restorations and similar things, schedule their work so they always have something to do and earn money. Even now, I will have more than one portrait in progress; switching back and forth can keep me fresh and, I had no doubt, that this was true for others.

So, when Alicia said she had an empty week, that didn't mean forty hours time three, but probably fifteen or twenty hours times three.

"Would you be able to bring them around tomorrow?" she asked.

"Sunday?"

"Yes. I've got some tidying up to do and an inventory, so if you could get them here, we can start first thing Monday."

There was no reason why I couldn't, so I agreed. If Marissa said no, then I could call Alicia and cancel.

Next, I called Sophie. As I suspected, she and April were just settling down with a gin and tonic.

"How did you get on with James Beech?" she asked.

"I'll tell you everything, but I should report to my client first, and I need to ask her for more money."

"It's Nigel. He needs to ask you for more money," I could hear Sophie relay to her.

"Tell him everything I have is his," I heard her say, with a laugh.

She took the phone.

"Darling!" Marissa exclaimed. "I was hoping you'd call."

"How's the site?"

"Well I think Inspector Covell is a bit of a dish," she said. "You could have some competition, but everything else is a drag. They've excavated quite a lot – more than we could have done in the time – and they are turning up more bones."

"Different people or the same bloke?" I asked.

"Only one, so far," she said. "They found a few more bits of jaw but no skull yet."

"Do they have a theory why it's spread all over?"

"I bat my eyes, but he still tells me nothing. It's driving Max furious."

"No, he wouldn't be happy with you flirting with the police."

"No! About not telling him anything else they found," she said. She was laughing hard now. "He knows there is a good number of metal finds as we'd been turning up every day, but they won't tell him or let him see them."

"Poor chap. Some good news," I began and told her about Powell and Beech's reactions. Knowing the pictures were genuine cheered her up and she agreed to the cleaning as long as I didn't let things get out of control.

She then passed the phone back to Sophie, who put on her seriously annoyed voice.

"I'm coming back tomorrow and I'm going to need to speak to you about Miss Gilliat."

I could hear both April and Marissa laughing in the background, but that was no assurance that Sophie didn't mean what she said.

"All I can say is that dinner better be good." Then her voice softened. "I'm looking forward to being home and seeing you."

℘

Sunday

Alicia Stephanini had her studio/workshop in one of the surviving warehouses on the old St Saviour's Dock. It was a very short walk from my studio, but I needed a taxi to convey the pictures. It took a bit of juggling and blocking the lift door to get all the paintings down to the lobby at the same time, but the taxi had no problem accommodating them.

I buzzed Alicia before paying the taxi, and she came down from her loft to help.

Once in her studio, I stacked the pictures against a wall and greeted her properly. While she made coffee, I sneaked a look at some of her work in progress. Pieces ranged from Victorian and modern paintings, porcelain figurines, and pieces of ceramic sculpture to stuffed fish and sports trophies.

"How many people do you employ?" I asked.

"Eight, but they're not all full time. There are others who I've worked with before who will buy time and space to do a particular job."

"How does that work?"

"Remarkably well," she said. "It means that at any one time we have a variety of experience, and we often ask each other's opinions about how to proceed. Everyone's qualified, but people have worked all over – from the Hermitage, the Prado, the Uffizi to the Met and a host of smaller museums and colleges."

"Do you have trainees?"

"Not more than one at a time, and they are very carefully vetted – that can cost as much as what they pay," she said. "They start out mixing paint, slip, or tidying up and gradually learn how to test varnishes for cleaning."

She handed me the coffee.

"What's the attrition rate?"

"About fifty percent," she said, with a shrug. "I've had one or two come back, though, when they've grown up a bit."

Alicia had cleared a large area on a central table, and I unwrapped the flower painting and placed it in front of her.

She put on magnifiers – hers were equipped with LED lights – and began scanning the picture.

I sat on a stool and let her work.

After about five minutes, she took a notebook and began writing.

"Let's have a look at the canvas," she said.

I helped her to flip it and returned to my stool.

She looked at the edges, the strainer, and took a small brush and, lifting a central support, brushed underneath it and considered what she'd found. She then looked at me, nodded, and I helped her turn it back.

She made some more notes.

"May I see the next one?"

I removed the flowers and put the portrait before her.

Before lowering her headset, I am sure she whispered, "*Santo cielo!*"

She repeated the process for the lady and the landscape. When she'd finished, she put the kettle on again, then sat on a stool near me.

"So, what do you want done?"

"These are not my pictures but when I saw them, I thought they should be investigated and to do that properly, I thought they should be cleaned," I said.

Alicia nodded.

"Before cleaning them, I also thought I should get a few opinions on whether they were what they pretended to be," I continued. "Rather than take these to the back door of one of the auction houses where – if they were genuine – word would be all around Bond and Dover Streets before I got home, I called two old friends, David

Powell and James Beech. They looked at them – separately – and confirmed that they thought they were real and deserved investigating.

"Of course, we discussed all sorts of possibilities, but you will have already seen that the portrait and the flowers have been in a fire," I said. "What do I want? I think for now, a cleaning and revarnish, but please save samples of the grime and old varnish. Just some cotton balls from each picture would be fine."

Alicia nodded.

"I brought them to you because I know you'll keep this confidential," I added.

"Where are you going to take them next?"

"To Helena Stirakis at the Courtauld."

"*È formidabile!*"

"Indeed."

"But a good move," Alicia added, reaching for a small pad of paper.

"Apart from the confidentiality, I want to say that you may delegate the work to anyone you trust to do it. I know you don't do it all yourself."

"Thank you," she said, and handed me the paper on which she had quoted for each picture and given the total.

"To be honest, I don't know if it will be possible to clean the portrait. The soot is baked into the paint, but we might be able to get the old varnish off, especially in the pendant area," she explained. "I will do that one myself. I'll try a section and if it goes badly, I'll stop, but once it's been seen by Dr Stirakis, we can make it look dirty again so it looks like it does now."

"*Perfetto.*"

We discussed a few more details before I left. She thought the cleaning and varnish removal could be done in a week and that she'd come in to varnish them in a week's time so I could have them the following Monday. This meant I could book an appointment with Helena early the following week and, in the meantime, get on with my neglected portraits.

I thought about walking back and having lunch at my club when I remembered that I promised to cook for Sophie that evening. So, it was the Jubilee Line from London Bridge to Green Park, after doing some shopping along the way.

Chapter Sixteen

Sunday

Sophie's return brought my world back to normal. I'd never let her know that, and I am sure she felt the same. She'd lived at Albany long enough for it to be hard to imagine her elsewhere. We'd passed the stage where we didn't mind telling each other we were busy and to go away and moved into the stage when we'd come in and sit down anyway.

Yet, the inevitable distance remained, and we accepted it.

Dinner would be a simple eggplant parmigiana, salad, garlic bread and a bottle of Corvo Rosso that I had managed to find.

At least she wouldn't have to drive home.

After setting out the things for supper, I made notes on the discussion I had with Alicia Stephanini. She had made no comment on the pieces except about their condition and what I proposed for their initial conservation. Remarkably, unless they had been previously restored, they displayed little paint loss and the canvases and panel were intact.

Supper wouldn't take long to prepare. I could see by the lights and curtains at Sophie's set that she had arrived

151

home and was probably having a long soak in a hot bath. I had a few hours to think and plan the next week.

There was work in progress that I needed to get back to, and I also needed to make my submissions to the Summer Exhibition. My portraits are big – as readers know – being a metre square – and the Royal Academy only allows RAs so many square feet, though we can submit up to six pictures. I entered every year; I felt it a duty to the academy, its supporters and to myself. If the critics – or worse – the public felt I was slipping, I wanted to know.

It's a funny thing, entering portraits in the Summer Exhibition. Apart from being Britain's foremost art event of the summer, it's also a huge marketplace for new and established buyers. However, portraits are seldom for sale. They've already been commissioned, bought and paid for, so in some ways, exhibiting there is merely an ego trip for both artist and subject.

I had chosen two and had consent to enter them. The first was a military portrait of a colonel who had distinguished himself in Afghanistan and had received a terrible wound on the right side of his face. His regiment had admired the man before his act of heroism and funded the portrait from clandestine collections.

Now retired, he had asked me to paint him against a background in Helmand for which he supplied photographs. The detail of military uniforms, badges, medals and ribbons has to be impeccable or the painting is forever ridiculed, so it took longer than average.

When discussing the pose, he said that he'd always considered his right his best side, so he wanted to be angled that way.

"And I want the scars painted as perfectly as the ribbons," he barked. "To do anything less would suggest I was ashamed of what I did."

Our sittings were fascinating, and I learned much. When I told him I'd been an officer in the Royal Navy many decades ago, his response was kind and flattering:

"You don't need to tell me that, sir. It's bloody obvious!"

Not known until now is that I sent the commission fee to the SSFA.

The second portrait is almost irreverent by comparison. It's a whimsical portrait of another painter who wanted to have some fun. While not *Dali Atomicus*, the artist's pose was playful, the shirt he wore could be described by a blind man as colourful, and there were objects about his studio in the background that weren't quite right: a clock with backwards numbers, a chair with a missing leg, a window with a missing muntin, a rug with a pattern that changes halfway along; and, as a nod to Brian Organ's portrait, *Diana, Princess of Wales*, the door has no knob. There are a few visual *double entendres* and in-jokes but we were both pleased with the result.

I always laugh when I see it, or a photograph of it, not because of the image itself, but of the fun the two of us had in its creation.

I credit Sophie with a sixth sense, for it is one of life's inevitabilities that when I put ice in a glass for a gin and tonic or pull a cork, she taps on my door.

I put the bottle down and let her in. She looked refreshed and restored to her London look.

"It's good to see you, darling!" she exclaimed, giving me the briefest of hugs and two air kisses.

"And you," I said. "Train on time?"

"Yes. Fine, but by the time I'd got a taxi and stumbled into my flat, I wasn't fit to be with."

"Set."

"Pedant, and yes, please, to a drink."

"I thought your bath would have relaxed you," I said. She shot me a look, but said nothing.

"How did you leave April, Marissa and the skeleton?" I mixed her drink while she settled into the sofa.

"Well, superficially, nothing's going on, but just below the surface, things are a bit more fraught. Max, frustrated with the loss of control over the dig, decamped this morning. However, the real reason is he didn't like watching Marissa making a play for Detective Inspector Covell."

"Ah. The makings of another murder at Bickering?"

Sophie laughed.

"You know what she's like," she said, lightly.

"I do," I said, with mock seriousness. "I feel – what's the word used these days? – *Dissed*. I shall drive right back up there, confront that bounder Covell, and tell him it's pistols at dawn."

Sophie was laughing so much that her drink was in danger.

"I don't know how many centuries you mixed up in that sentence," she managed to say. "You can relax, though, my darling, Inspector Covell shows no signs of being enamoured with your Marissa. He's very courteous and respectful, but I have the sense he treats everyone that way.

"He interviewed me – very briefly – since I'd found the bullet and jaw fragment. I was no more than Sophie Gregg; he had no idea I'm anything more than April's friend."

I supposed it was possible that someone might not recognise her, but I wasn't sure.

I freshened our drinks and went to the kitchen to put the casserole in the oven and pull the cork.

"Haven't you looked at your post since you got back?" Sophie called.

"Reading my mail again? I think there's a law against that."

I returned to the sitting room.

Sophie was tapping a blue envelope on her fingertips.

"It's from Lincolnshire, but it's not April's schoolgirl scrawl, nor is it Marissa's writing – I can read it," she teased, "so who else do you know in Lincolnshire."

"It's probably the hotel restaurant bill," I said.

If she wanted to tease, I could, too.

"On blue paper?"

"Someone from the dig wanting to see their sketch."

Sophie considered this.

"No, I don't think it's that."

"I'll look at it later," I said.

"Aren't you curious?"

"Yes, I am," I conceded, "but I'm more hungry than curious. The first course is on the table."

Our conversation turned to what we'd be doing in the coming week. Sophie had some appearances, meetings with her agent and the director of her next production.

We talked about people, and I suggested that she might enjoy meeting David and Madeline Powell. Sophie had been a regular customer at Madeline's shops in her teens and twenties and was fascinated by the story about her brother.

"Madeline appears intimidating, but she thaws quickly," I said.

"How did she meet David Powell?"

"He'd known her through her brother. They worked at the same newspaper for a while, but they became close after her brother's death," I said. "He helped her sort his things. She will tell you more, if she wants to."

"Intriguing."

Sophie had eaten the casserole without comment, but seemed surprised when I placed a small dish of vanilla ice cream before her. The look clearly said, "Is this all?"

I then retrieved a bottle of Tia Maria from the sideboard.

"Pour this on, it will make you happier."

She took the bottle and smiled.

"You're not getting me drunk – again," she said, with a look of warning.

"When have I *ever* done that?" I asked, feigning offence.

"No, you're right. You just drive me to drink."

♋

After the initial teasing, our conversation returned to normal, but Sophie shared no worries or confidences. As she had said, she wanted an early night and left my set just before nine. She had not returned to the subject of the blue letter that still lay on the coffee table with the other bills.

Once I cleared the kitchen, I poured the rest of the wine and slit it open.

It was a good thing that I hadn't opened it as it had come from Rachel Rawding, and I wouldn't have heard the end of it for the rest of the evening.

Dear Sir Nigel,

Though I have only a passing interest in art, I have known your work for a long time, partly through my parents and my own reading and gallery visits, but also through another connection which will have to be a subject of a future conversation.

I would like to ask if you'd consider doing a portrait of me. I don't know if you paint ordinary people, but for a variety of reasons, I think I would like it done.

I think the one you did of Marissa is excellent and also the one of Sophie Gregg/Ligeia Gordon, though I have only seen pictures of that one. Spending time with both of them and meeting you has been the catalyst for this letter.

If you let me know a good time to telephone you, we can discuss it further. If you don't want to paint me, I'll get over it!

Sincerely,

Rachel (Rawding)

Chapter Seventeen

Monday

I walked to the studio and began a very normal week. I had only one sitting, an architect, on Wednesday, and the other days would be taken up with the dig water-colours and sketches and advancing the portraits in progress.

Around lunch time, I called Rachel on the number she'd given and left a message with my studio number.

I then set to work on the watercolours.

The medium is so different from oils that one has to change gear totally. A painter friend said it was like going from driving to flying. You're still trying to get from one place to another, but the operation of an aeroplane is considerably different to that of a car.

I began by selecting a palette. I thought if the paintings were to be a series, I ought to use the same colours in each. The idea then came to me to do them with what's known as a "limited palette," that is one where only four or five colours are used to create a spectrum that is distinct to an artist or set of pictures.

Probably the most famous limited palette was that of the Swedish painter, Anders Zorn. The idea was also picked up by Sargent who had experimented using a different set of colours, depending on the subject.

It's an act of pure vanity to imitate those legends, and one of arrogance to create my own limited colour set. However, for the dig, I needed good earths, brick reds, and good greys. While Zorn's palette was limited to four colours, I resolved not to be dogmatic, but would try to keep things under control.

Working primarily in oils meant that my stock of watercolours was limited anyway. I decided to experiment in building a palette based on alizarin crimson, lemon yellow, ultramarine and ivory black. My concern was that I couldn't get the greens I wanted from those colours, but I'd just have to see. Adding white was another option.

The first step was to build a colour chart using a system built on the Mendel square with swatches of all four colours down the side of the paper and again across the top. Next was to mix each colour down the side with those across the top until the square was complete.

Of course, the tones could be adjusted and diluted in infinite proportions, but beyond the basic mix, it was better simply to buy a tube of the desired colour.

I sat at the table and began constructing the chart and was halfway through the twelve colours when the telephone rang. I decided to let it go to voice mail and continued working.

However, when I heard Rachel Rawding's voice, I stopped and picked up.

"Good morning, Mrs Rawding," I said, catching her before she finished her message.

"I'm sorry, I'm obviously interrupting," she said.

"It's all right, I asked you to call."

"You obviously got my note," she began. "Will you paint me?"

Her question was both confident and innocent. I like people who know what they want and can articulate it. Having had such a brutal experience of death, she would be sensitive to the fragility of life and ensure that she was not wasting time.

"Yes, I will, subject to a few parameters – nothing onerous, just practicalities."

"Good, thank you," she said. "What are your parameters?"

"I usually explain these in person, but since you're in Lincolnshire, we can do it by phone, unless you want me to email the questions."

"That's one of the reasons I wrote to you when I did," she said. "I'm coming down to London on Thursday and will be there until Sunday afternoon."

"Could you come to my studio Friday at around ten? It's in Southwark, not far from London Bridge Station. I'll email you the address."

She agreed and said goodbye without any further questions or gossip.

Two things came to mind: how would she want to be painted, and how would I tell Sophie.

For the remainder of the morning, I continued work on the watercolours, completing the chart and making a good start on the first picture.

After a quick lunch at a local shop that did sandwiches, wraps, rolls and other meals that involved putting different types of food on different types of bread, I spent the afternoon working on one of my unfinished portraits.

On the way home, I realised that I hadn't given Marissa's paintings a thought all day, and wondered how Alicia was getting on with them. With paintings that old, there was a lot that could go wrong. Significant amounts of over-painting from earlier restorations could come off taking period details with it. Worse, original paint could come off if the chemicals used were wrong or too strong. Another hazard was that rips or punctures in the canvas would be revealed – though no one had seen any signs of them. In the case of the portrait, the thousands of tiny areas of paint formed by the fire could just float off, or be torn off by the balls of cotton used to apply the solvents.

This sort of work took a lot of trust, from Marissa to me, from me to Alicia. Everyone involved hoped that the trust would be warranted.

❧

Wednesday

I saw Sophie for a quick drink Tuesday night before she went to some function. The limited time available made it a good opportunity to tell her about Rachel Rawding's note and telephone call.

In what I considered a masterful move, I invited her to come to the studio Friday morning, too, and then join us for lunch. This gave her little time to object as well as a chance to see someone I suspected she liked.

With Sophie mollified, I was able to get on with the rest of my week. There had been no calls from Alicia to say that any of the paintings had disappeared with the removal of the varnish, nor any messages from Lincolnshire on the progress – or not – of the police.

Commissions to paint architects aren't frequent but they tend to come from colleges and universities where they might have studied, an institution with a significant building they had designed, a museum from their home city, or the architects themselves.

I know many will condemn me, but I have refused to paint architects whose buildings I hate. I have endeavoured to ameliorate the amount of ugliness in the world, not celebrate it.

I liked the buildings of Nicholas Goffin so had no qualms about painting him. The hallmark of his buildings was they always fit their surroundings. To give you an idea of what I mean, have a look at Sir William Whitfield's building at 79 Whitehall. Originally designed for the Department of Health, it was renovated to be occupied by Parliament during the renovation of the Pugin building.

Seventy-nine Whitehall takes cues from the surrounding architecture and from Jacobean buildings but with a distinctive contemporary modality, as the pretentious critics would put it.

Goffin's other buildings displayed similar sensitivity and blended chameleon-like with Tudor, Georgian, Victorian, Art Deco and other styles. His other great trick was that these buildings were distinctive in their own right. There were subtle – but detectable – characteristics that made it possible to identify a Goffin building.

Goffin was a man of Chestertonian proportions. The first impression was that he was intimidating, possibly impatient, and he certainly regarded me as he might a building he did not like.

On his first visit, we discussed how he would like to be painted. I had printed pictures of his major buildings should he want one or more in the background of his portrait, but he asked if he could be shown working at a traditional drawing board with plans, compasses, dividers, a prismatic scale, mechanical pencil and a plain rubber.

As we talked, he revealed an affability that I hadn't suspected. I had drawn some sketches from a three-quarter view that showed the objects with him standing at a drafting table wearing spectacles, suit and tie.

He picked one of the sketches and pronounced that to be the one he wanted painted.

"I don't suppose I could have an antique wooden drafting table with cast iron legs," he asked, like a child asking for an ice cream.

"I'll see what I can do."

By the second sitting, I had found some photographs of the table, complete with spoked hand wheels and painted it in roughly. From that moment, he would have stood on his head had I asked him.

The picture was all but done. We had settled for a simple modern office scene in the background with one disturbance: outside the large window on the side wall was not a cityscape, but a Daliesque flat plain with converging lines stretching into the distance. He liked the joke and hoped others might get it.

By the time he left, only some fine tuning and refinements were needed, so we could have "Varnishing Day" the following week. If I worked on it Thursday, it would be complete before Rachel Rawding came. It would delay work on the watercolours, but they weren't time-critical.

I had a boyish curiosity about how the police were getting on, whether the old pistol was a murder weapon and if the bones showed signs of murder.

Who would be the best to solve this case? Adam Dalgleish? Inspector Morse? Father Brown?

All things considered, I think I'd opt for Peter Wimsey.

Chapter Eighteen

Friday

Nicholas Goffin's portrait was finished. All that was left was to show it to him, make any final adjustments and have a glass of champagne. It made a good statement and captured the meticulous professionalism of the man as well as something of his humour.

I had the studio tidied before Rachel Rawding's arrival. There were no portraits on view, and my paints and palette were put away. Only my sketchbook and pencils were to hand.

I was expecting the door buzzer to ring, so the telephone surprised me. For a moment I thought it would be Rachel cancelling her appointment, but it was Alicia.

"The cleaning is finished," she said. "There were no disasters. I'm going to varnish them today – I've done one already – so you can pick them up at about one tomorrow."

She caught a hesitancy in my voice. I was debating whether to ask how they looked, but she thought I wanted to pick them up later.

"Please pick them up tomorrow," she said, with a laugh. "They are covering all my flat surfaces."

167

And then the door buzzer sounded. I pressed the release, told Alicia I'd see her shortly after lunch and went onto the landing to meet the lift.

"Sir Nigel!" Rachel said, brightly as she stepped forward.

I motioned her to the door of the studio, and followed her in. She didn't make the usual, "It doesn't look like a studio," comment, but quietly looked around and considered the few pictures on my walls.

"Have you started the watercolours?" she asked, after wandering around the whole room while I made coffee.

I took her coat and put it on the bed in the other room.

"Yes, but there have been a few distractions. Have a seat."

I put the coffee on the table near her then sat in my armchair and picked up my sketch pad. I waited a few minutes for her to begin speaking, but she seemed suddenly intimidated.

"Are you aware of any developments at the dig?" I asked, opening the pad and making a few lines.

"Members of the force have let the odd thing slip, because they knew my husband, not because I worked on the dig," she said. "All I know is that they expect to have the site excavated down to the floor by the end of today; that they have not yet found the whole skeleton, and that it seems to be too old to have been killed by the 1851 Navy Colt."

I smiled.

"That's quite a bit. According to Sophie, Marissa doesn't know that much," I said.

Rachel looked embarrassed.

"Perhaps I shouldn't have said anything," she replied, then laughed. "Oh, it's not as though it were an on-going crime investigation. I think the information is restricted because they don't want to be hampered by tourists."

I nodded.

"Any theories?"

"One idea was that the enclosure was used as a piggery and stuff would just be dumped there."

"You'd think a corpse, dismembered or not, would be noticed," I said.

"What do I know? I'm an English teacher – or was at least."

"Tell me about the portrait you'd like."

Rachel's demeanour was different from that I had seen in Lincolnshire. She lacked confidence; perhaps it was being in an unfamiliar environment. Many people were anxious about having a professional photographic portrait taken which takes a fraction of a second. Posing for hours of continuous scrutiny is something far less usual today.

169

"Do you think I'm very vain?" she asked. "I'm no one special."

She paused.

"Maybe this was a bad idea," she added.

I put the sketchpad down and picked up my coffee.

"Rachel, what made you want to have your portrait painted?"

She looked down, embarrassed, then looked up and met my eye.

"I saw Marissa's picture and thought how wonderful it would be to be remembered by something like that," she said, her confidence regained. "After seeing it, I looked at some of your other pictures online."

She smiled, "It's a bit silly as I only have a small cottage."

"That shouldn't be a factor," I replied. "Sophie was living in a tiny space in Muswell Hill when she had her portrait painted. I think she moved to Albany just to get enough wall space. She'd been in the Muswell Hill flat for decades."

Rachel's eyes opened.

"She doesn't live in a penthouse or luxury flat overlooking the river?"

"She's a very modest lady," I said. "She wasn't putting on a Marie-Antoinette peasant act at the dig."

"So, she *is* an old university friend of April?" she asked, hardly believing it. "She was very nice, but I was almost afraid to speak to her. Once you got there, she only wanted to talk to April and you."

"Did it come across like that? I'll have to speak to her."

I stood and went to the telephone and dialled as Rachel regarded me with suspicion.

"It's me, Sophie. As planned. One o'clock."

I hung up and sat down with Rachel still staring at me.

"Sophie's joining us for lunch. You can slay your dragon, lay to rest a ghost, or whatever," I said, picking up the pad again. "Now can we get back to the portrait?"

"It's as I said," she said, recovering herself. "I want to leave something lasting behind. When Paul was killed, mortality hit me in the face."

"You were very young – you still are."

"I don't feel young."

She thought about that.

"So, the portrait is for you, for now. What would you like to wear? What image do you wish to portray, and what are your favourite colours?"

Her first answers were very tentative, but I kept prodding.

"Do you want to stand or sit? Do you want to be doing something active – read, write, play the piano, dig your garden, stand in front of a class?"

This got a genuine laugh.

"With a clicker in my hand and a bit of Shakespearean text on the white board?"

"For some reason, Shelley just came to mind," I said, having a sudden indefinable insight. "Do you like him?"

"I find the story of his life more interesting than his poetry."

I chuckled.

"I don't think you'll find yourself alone in that," I said.

"You know poetry?" she asked, surprised.

"I had several exceedingly boring years on a ship in the Royal Navy," I said. "I wasn't good at much, so I had lots of time to read."

"I think that's almost true," Rachel replied, with a canny look. "Why Shelley?"

"I never could remember more than first lines of most things, but just for a second, it reminded me of the line, 'We are as clouds that veil the midnight moon.'"

Rachel looked surprised and was silent for a moment.

"That is a very haunting line," she said. "But what has it to do with my portrait?"

"Would you like to be painted by moonlight?"

∽

Sophie knocked on the door at almost precisely one o'clock. Rachel had relaxed as we explored the idea of a moonlight portrait, and I made studies of her hands, eyes, ears and mouth as we talked. I had also been able to rough out several possible compositions. The one she liked best was one that showed her striding towards the viewer along a garden path with an old brick wall to her left and a bank of untamed flowers to her right.

It had been difficult to articulate her ideas, but Rachel liked the literary connection as well as the partial freedom of being outdoors but with a *mysterioso* atmosphere.

Sophie's arrival provided a total break from the concentration I had demanded of Rachel, and she relaxed instantly, but was soon overwhelmed by the presence of Dame Ligeia Gordon.

Sophie was used to this and took Rachel by the arm and led her from the studio. I washed the mugs and put the sketchpad away, turned out the lights and locked up.

On the pavement, I watched Sophie and Rachel walking ahead of me. Sophie was chatting easily, and Rachel seemed to be more relaxed. Sophie knew where I'd be going, so there was no need to rush to catch up.

Rather than wait for me, they went straight to a table and Sophie was talking animatedly when I joined them. She continued as I sat down, but Rachel felt she should recognise my presence.

"Sophie was telling me about the day she came to see you to ask for her portrait to be painted," she explained. "She said she was terrified."

I put my glasses on to read the menu.

"Oh, did she, now?" I said. "I don't remember it quite that way."

Sophie looked at me as if to say, "Don't ruin a good story." That might not have been exactly it, but the "Don't" was clear.

"Have you decided what to wear?" Sophie asked.

"I have some ideas," Rachel said. "Will he make me wear something else?"

"Who knows? Nigel is incredibly predictable until he isn't," Sophie replied, mischievously.

"I think you'd better look at the menu," I said.

We had a very enjoyable meal. It was one of the rare ones when no one recognised Sophie, or if they did, they didn't come to talk to her. The conversation had left portraiture behind, explored aspects of the dig, and had moved to Sophie and me comparing diaries for the coming week.

"Rather than trek back and forth to Lincolnshire, would you like me to paint your portrait in a week of consecutive two-hour sittings? You could stay in London," I suggested.

"When were you thinking?" Rachel asked.

"The week after next," I said.

"Remember we're having lunch with Bill and Virginia on Wednesday," Sophie said.

"That's okay, we can do the sitting that day from nine to eleven instead of ten to twelve," I said.

Rachel had gone pale and looked concerned.

"I knew a Bill and Virginia," she said, very softly.

"Bill Warren's an old friend of Nigel's from Cambridge rowing days," Sophie explained.

"And he worked for Scotland Yard?" Rachel asked, hesitantly.

"He's been retired some time," I said.

Sophie and I looked at her. She appeared to have shrunk in size and her voice could barely be heard above that of the restaurant.

"He was wounded in the same incident in which my husband was killed."

176

Chapter Nineteen

Friday

ophie and I sat there, dumbstruck. Rachel stared at us for a moment and murmured, "I'm sorry," before standing up.

Sophie reached out to her, catching her arm.

"It's all right, Rachel. Sit down," she said, softly.

She sat, and Sophie continued:

"We had no idea that Bill had been injured," she said. "He's never mentioned it, and neither has Virginia. Did you know anything, darling?"

The use of an expression of endearment in public demonstrated the depth of Sophie's surprise. I tried to remember the time when the incident might have taken place, but nothing came to mind, though Bill and I could go for months without contact.

"I'm so sorry," Rachel repeated.

"Rachel, you have nothing to be sorry about," Sophie said. "We didn't lose a spouse – or even a friend."

Rachel was upset, but it did seem to be for us, not for her own loss.

"This was supposed to be fun, a celebration lunch, not a wake," she said, recovering herself. "I came to terms with Paul's death a long time ago. You really didn't know about Chief Inspector Warren being injured?"

"It's not like Bill to draw attention to himself," I said. "I can imagine losing a man on one of his operations affected him deeply."

Rachel looked concerned, but a little confused.

"It wasn't his operation," she said. "They both were working with one of Chief Inspector Warren's superiors – not that I imagine there were many."

This rang a distant bell – something about a raid going pear-shaped and a senior officer (who must have been Bill's boss) being "reassigned." Bill must have been the "another officer" in the newspapers. I'd never associated Bill with the operation. I was also surprised that he and Virginia had been able to keep such a tight lid on it.

"Paul admired the chief inspector very much," she was saying, when I began listening again.

"Such a small world," Sophie said.

"Yes, it is," Rachel agreed. "The police circle is fairly small, as I imagine the Cambridge one is – possibly even the Royal Navy."

"It is," I agreed, "but generally only among those who made careers of it. I was well-treated while I was in – and my commanding officer engineered my entry to Cambridge."

Sophie leaned towards Rachel and spoke in a stage whisper:

"It was mostly the Jesuits, and circles seldom get smaller and tighter than that."

Rachel laughed.

In spite of the sad subject, we'd all recovered our good humour.

We finished our meal and coffee. I promised I'd have some preliminary ideas for Rachel when she came in ten days' time. She formally shook our hands, thanked us and said goodbye.

"Where is she staying?" Sophie asked.

"I have no idea."

৪৩

On our walk back, Sophie returned to the matter of Bill's wounding.

"I can't understand why Virginia didn't tell us," she repeated. "Don't you wonder about Bill not telling you? You must be one of his oldest friends."

"He'd have told me if he wanted to," I said.

Sophie looked furious.

"Don't you care that one of your friends was probably nearly killed?"

"Of course, I do," I said. "But, if he wants to keep it private, that's up to him."

We'd just crossed Golden Jubilee Bridge before Sophie was ready to speak to me again.

"Rachel's quite lovely in an unconventional way," she said. "How are you going to paint her?"

"I thought I might paint her in the moonlight," I said.

"Outside?"

"Her or me?"

Sophie gave me one of her tolerant looks.

"I'll do the painting inside," I said, giving her a smile. "You have given me an idea. I had been thinking of painting her outside, but you've reminded me of one of Tina Spratt's paintings."

I hadn't thought of it before, but the painting "Candle Light" had a figure illuminated by both warm candle light and cool moonlight, creating a feeling of ambiguity in an already intriguing setting. In "Candle Light" the figure is near an unseen window or door that is admitting the light. How, I wondered, would Rachel Rawding look near a window the viewer could see?

I realised I had been silent for some time and that Sophie would be wondering what I was thinking about. She had just accepted Rachel, and I didn't want to upset that disposition.

"Have you got anything on tomorrow afternoon?" I ventured.

"Might do."

"Late lunch?"

She smiled and nodded.

"Something of a working lunch?" I added.

"I figured there would be strings," she replied, with a laugh.

I told her about collecting the pictures from Alicia. She was clearly enthusiastic about seeing the pictures but still made a disparaging comment about enlisting a BAFTA-award winning dame as a baggage handler.

"That's the key to your success, Sophie: you're versatile."

ೞ

Saturday

Given the choice of an early or late lunch, Sophie chose a late one. We took the Underground to Bermondsey and walked to St Saviour's Dock. Sophie didn't know this area, and walking from Bermondsey rather than London Bridge – which was about the same distance – gave her a feel for the place.

"Do you know if Alicia found anything?" she asked.

"No," I said. "She simply said they'd be ready for collection today."

"It will be interesting to see what has been revealed. I suppose it's possible that they were in the cupboard for a good reason."

Alicia had a curious combination of friendliness and formality. When there was business to be discussed, she was as professional as the stuffiest of art historians but in social conversations, her Italian exuberance was irrepressible.

I introduced her to Sophie, adding that she might know her as Ligeia Gordon. I could have been introducing her to a relative. She embraced her, kissed her cheeks and complimented her on a favourite stage role.

For once, Sophie was taken aback, but warmed to Alicia.

"I have heard nothing but praise for *your* work," Sophie said, attempting to reflect Alicia's enthusiasm.

Alicia then turned and led us into the studio; as she did, her manner changed to the professional.

The paintings were laid flat on the large central table. Already I could see the colours pop.

She began with the portrait.

"You will see, Sir Nigel, that this one is unchanged. I attempted to clean a small section down in the left corner where her arm is. Unfortunately, the varnish is baked into the paint along with the soot. The cupping, as you know is severe, and it makes rubbing the surface virtually impossible – the danger of a cotton swab catching and lifting the tessellated paint off is too great to risk.

"The pearl over-painting was very crude and came off easily and cleanly," she said. "It was strange."

"Strange?"

Alicia nodded.

"It was as though it was a temporary covering, not meant to last. It was painted over a layer of wax which made it easy to lift and remove."

We looked at the image, which even in its degraded condition, was fascinating.

"Is there nothing that can be done? It's such an attractive face," Sophie asked.

It was unlike Sophie to enter my "professional" discussions, but she had seen the picture before I had and clearly felt some proprietary responsibility and interest.

"If it were to be restored, it could be chemically treated to make the paint lie flat and stabilised. It could then be restored, but you might end up with ninety per cent restoration and only ten per cent original," she said. "It rather depends what they want to do with it."

We looked at the unknown lady in silence for several minutes, wondering who she was and what was her history. Had she been in the fire, or was that after her death?

"These flowers, on the other hand," Alicia said, moving us around the table, "have come up beautifully. The colours are vibrant, it is in good condition – it has not been relined and does not appear to have been restored. The Courtauld can confirm that. There is only a small area of paint loss down in the lower right corner. It's just black background, but it may have had a signature there, which is frustrating."

"That's beautiful!" I exclaimed. "You can practically pick one up."

"It's very good," Alicia agreed. "Something to ask Dr Stirakis: I'm not particularly good at flowers, but it would be interesting to know if all of these would have been in flower at the same time.

"There's one other thing," she added, before I could say that Beech had made the same observation. "While there was no blistering or damage from the fire, there was soot all over it. I've saved some swabs from both the portrait and this one in the event that someone wants to try to determine whether it was the same fire or a different one."

"Perhaps the flowers were in a different room?" I suggested.

"That could explain it."

The question about the blossoms being in flower at the same time was an excellent one. Seeing the cleaned version renewed the feeling that I was missing something that I had when I first examined it.

"Finally," Alicia said, moving us on to the next picture, "is the landscape. Again, there has been some paint loss, but not in any critical areas. While not my department, this painting is much later and has no signs of fire or smoke damage. Plenty of nicotine and normal household wood and coal smoke and grease, but nothing catastrophic.

"If asked to venture a guess as to its location, I'd suggest a public house. There were splashes of liquids on it as well as the smoke. Possibly even some flakes of long dried food.

"I expect you'll get a slap on the wrist from the lovely Helena for not letting her team clean these," Alicia continued, "but it won't have made much difference. As you noted, there was nothing to suggest these were anything artistically special – but that's not my department, either."

The laughter that followed this comment signalled that she was done.

I spent another few moments looking at the landscape to see if there were something to give a clue as to its place. However, apart from ruin and thatched farm buildings, there was nothing. No towers or spires on the horizon, no lakes, ponds or rivers, no significant houses – or pubs – but the sunset was more dazzling than ever.

I helped Alicia wrap the pictures while Sophie called for a taxi. We'd take the pictures back to my studio and then go to lunch.

I was entirely satisfied with the cleaning and re-varnishing. The pictures certainly looked better, and Marissa would be able to hang them again if she wanted. I'd learned nothing more but felt that the process would assist Helena Stirakis in her examination.

Sophie seemed surprised at my lack of overt excitement, but all the main questions remained, and I wasn't the one who would be able to answer them.

Chapter Twenty

Tuesday

At the Courtauld, several picture handlers took the larger paintings from the taxi while I carried the small portrait. I didn't have to wait long for Dr Stirakis to appear. She directed the head porter, Guy Stone, to put the pictures on a trolley and take them up to her studio.

After our last, less than satisfactory encounter, I feared that Helena wouldn't give me – or these paintings – the time I felt they deserved. However, she greeted me warmly and watched with anticipation as I unwrapped the portrait.

When I saw her eyes widen, I knew things would go well.

"Where did this come from?" she asked.

Her voice was little more than a whisper.

"Your reaction was much the same as mine," I said. "A house in Lincolnshire. It's been in the back of a cupboard for at least two hundred years."

"Poor thing. The damage is bad, but the face is surprisingly clear."

"That was my thought," I said. "Alicia Stephanini cleaned and revarnished the other two, but only attempted a square centimetre or two on this one."

I indicated the area in the corner and around the pendant.

"She was wise to stop," she said.

She went to get her magnifying headset and returned to study the image.

After a while, I asked:

"Do you recognise her?"

"No."

"Is she as old as she looks?"

She turned the panel over carefully and looked.

"Absolutely nothing," she said, ignoring the question. "The panel is good. The cut and finish marks are consistent with the period."

"James Beech thought it might be larch."

"Beech? You dragged him out again?" Helena asked, raising her headset and turning to me.

"I don't know that many people in the fraud identification game – and they've all retired."

Helena laughed. She was much more relaxed than the last time I consulted her.

"We'll run the usual tests, but this looks real," she said. "I'll have the period experts look at it, too."

I decided not to quiz her about the white boar. I'd wait to see what developed.

"Beech suggested anything from 1525 to 1575 for this, but admitted his inexpertise."

Helena laughed easily.

"I'd say that was about right. If pushed, I'd guess 1550."

"Edward VI."

"Nasty times," she said. "He and his father were responsible for the destruction of most of British art. The majority of it was religious, but they were pretty indiscriminate. Later, the Puritans were blamed – which is still commonly believed – but they only mopped up another five per cent."

"Then you will be interested in this one," I said, unwrapping the flower painting.

If Helena Stirakis had been surprised by the portrait, she was confounded by this one.

She scrutinised it with her headset, then found a linen tester to have a closer look.

"I'm going to have to get several opinions on this one," she said, eventually. "If it is what I think it is, it shouldn't exist."

She stood up and looked at it from a distance.

"I want to see this on the easel," she said, as she rolled a studio easel to the table.

I helped her secure it.

She looked at the back.

"Nothing," she said. "Did Beech have a time period for this one?"

"Yes. 1550 to 1600."

She nodded. "I'd say 1575 to 1600, but not after. We'll know when we've had a better look."

"Alicia said she thought it had been in the same fire as the portrait."

"I'll say this, Nigel, you always seem to upset things."

I began unwrapping the landscape.

"You can relax. This is less interesting than the other two," I said. "Beech reckons this is late eighteenth century – possibly a little later. Probably by a local amateur or itinerant painter. Alicia thinks it might have been a pub judging by the nicotine, grease and smoke on it. I have some swabs from each of the paintings."

I handed her an envelope from my jacket pocket.

"They're labelled."

Helena nodded and wrote on the envelope.

"Do you know where this is?"

"No. I suspect its in Lincolnshire, but it will take local knowledge to recognise it."

"Initially, I'd agree with everything you've said, but we'll see."

◌

Wednesday

The finalisation of Nicholas Goffin's portrait went smoothly. He was pleased with the way the elements had come together and over champagne continued the discussions we'd had about architecture and place. I found him very modest about his ability but outspoken about architecture.

"There are architects who pretend that what we do is a fine art, but it isn't," he pronounced. "It's an applied art, and more and more, it's an applied science with art taking second place.

"The fine art nonsense began with the publication of Diderot's *Encyclopédie*. D'Alembert wrote the section on architecture and called it a fine art – he was a mathematician – what would *he* know? Since then, you've had all sorts of idiots poncing about making silly statements about putting up functional buildings."

While Goffin had moments of hyperbole, he was also able to have very human conversations about how dreadful it was to work in a cubicle in buildings where the windows don't open.

"When the power plants get shut down and the move away from fossil fuels is finished, there will be energy rationing until the technology catches up," he said. "Waiting for lifts in anything over fifteen stories is a nightmare already, but power shortages could easily make tall buildings uninhabitable."

When the champagne was gone, he suggested going to lunch.

"Come with me," he said, and set off down the street.

For a large man, he moved quickly, lightly stepping down the escalators in the Underground and navigating the interchanges until we emerged at Piccadilly and headed up Dean Street.

I thought the Groucho Club an incongruous place for Goffin, but once we entered, I saw it suited him perfectly. He knew many of the members we encountered and were frequently interrupted over lunch by people who wanted to say a little more than hello.

"Nearest thing to the Drones Club I could find," he said.

∞

Sophie was back from her read-through when I returned to Albany. The lunch hadn't been particularly alcoholic, but the conversation afterwards had been fascinating and jovial, and it was nearly three thirty when I looked at my watch.

"Aren't you getting a bit old for that sort of thing?" Sophie scolded. "You'll be throwing bread rolls next."

"How was your read through?" I asked, there was no point in rising to that bait.

"These things are always very informative," she said. "You learn very quickly who can't act and that the director has no understanding of what the play's about."

"How can you not understand *Relative Values*?"

"Oh, don't ask," Sophie replied, waving the question away. "Now that you've finished Christopher Wren's portrait, and Dr Stirakis has Marissa's paintings, what are you going to do before Rachel comes down next week?"

"I have the watercolours, which are getting pushed back even further, and there's a judge I have to finish off."

Sophie laughed.

"That sounds murderous. Do you want me to be your alibi?"

"No, thank you, you'd get the giggles."

"I beg your pardon!" Sophie exclaimed. "Are you suggesting that I couldn't perform a simple role as a lying accomplice?"

"Yes," I said, barely lifting my gaze. "You're a terrible liar."

"Am not!"

She was smiling now.

"Okay, see if you can slip a lie passed me in the next half hour."

&

I finished off the judge by Friday morning and completed two watercolours, too.

Spring was evident, even in the middle of London, and spring blossoms were appearing in the parks and squares. It was still a long way from being warm, but the longer days and frequent showers were convincing evidence that winter had passed.

On Saturday afternoon, Sophie and I ventured up to Hampstead and after a walk on the Heath, we went for tea at Louis'. It remained similar to the red-signed tearoom that I first knew fifty years before. It still served tea, coffee and delicious pastries, but no longer did the waiter – dressed like one in a Paris café – come round with a tray of samples to tempt you.

In the seventies, it was a place where you'd find a lot of people from the music industry. I think there must have been some recording studios in the area. From episodes of eavesdropping on conversations over the years, I gathered that these were technicians and the odd producer, sometimes accompanied by members of the backing groups, but not present nor future stars.

Their conversation was always relaxed, often technical. Usually, they displayed all the signs of people who had worked together for years, if not continuously. I gathered they'd come together for a time, then disperse. I saw them often enough that a few would say hello and pass a few words, but I don't think I ever had an extended conversation with any of them.

They created an animated, happy sounding background to tea, unlike many of the tea shops in London (off the tourist routes) that were filled with silent crowds, alone, or just not speaking. They also added a welcome masculine element.

I only ever went up to Hampstead a few times a year and for several decades it was a bitter-sweet experience as it had been a favourite place of my late wife, Vera. Taking Sophie there for the first time was difficult, though I was able to rationalise that I wasn't in love with Sophie. Now, it's just a place we go from time to time.

"I never realised I was such a bad liar," she said, drinking her cup of White Tea Silver Needle while I opted for Russian Caravan (without the Lapsang Souchong element).

"I can just tell when you're acting," I said. "Anyway, saying that Rachel called you was pretty obvious. She'd never dare."

Sophie shrugged and took a bite of her Florentine.

"Now, if you had said Marissa called, not only would I have believed you, but you'd have the bonus of terrifying me."

She laughed.

"I should call April and see if they're any further with the police investigation," she said. "I wonder if they'll ever start again."

We speculated idly about the resumption of work, the age of the skeleton, the purpose of the building and what Helena Stirakis might turn up about Marissa's paintings.

However, Sophie finally said what was really on her mind.

"Do you think I'm eccentric?"

The question came from nowhere, but I knew this was something she'd been brooding about.

"Not compared to your friends."

She gave me her patient look.

"No," I said, seriously. "I'd call you playful, but only with people you know understand your humour, and never about serious things."

Rather than ask why she asked, I waited. I nibbled on a thin vanilla wafer, aware that Sophie was staring at me.

"Is that all you have to say?"

I waited until I finished eating.

"I thought that was fairly accurate, not to mention flattering."

Her eyes were wide.

"Aren't you the least bit curious to know why I asked that question?"

"Yes, but you'll tell me when you're ready."

Whatever her instincts, she held back. She knew that if she pushed it, I'd say something to the effect that only people who were married would put up with such oblique communication.

"The director of *Relative Values* wants me to play Lady Marshwood as an eccentric," she finally revealed. "There's nothing eccentric about her. In fact, much of her comedy comes from her not being eccentric."

It was the sort of request that a young director who felt he had to do something different would try.

"I expect you're right, but you usually put up with such adolescent nonsense," I said.

Sophie sighed and leaned back in her chair.

"It's not that," she said. "It's what he said next."

She stared at me, daring me to ask.

I nodded encouragement, which seemed to suffice.

"He said, 'That should suit you very well.'"

"What did you say?"

"Nothing. A few sycophants laughed, but those who knew me didn't."

She thought for a moment.

"I'm an actress. I do what I'm told, but this is just so obviously wrong for the play it could seriously affect the whole thing and everyone else's roles."

That was one of the things that made Sophie – Ligeia Gordon – great. To her, "the play's the thing" wasn't just an empty phrase. It meant the play is important, and each person's role is important.

There's no doubt that in the United States, Ligeia Gordon is considered "a star." Here, she is simply "a leading actress" – one of many. She walks to the theatres, uses public transport, eats in ordinary restaurants, and takes tea with jobbing portrait painters. Were she in the U.S., it would all be stretch limos and thugs.

"What are you going to do?"

"I haven't figured that out yet, but I'll do something."

಄

We returned to Albany around five-thirty, and I made a quick change and freshened up and headed to Farm Street for the six o'clock Mass. I told Sophie I'd meet her for drinks and supper afterwards.

197

The church was peaceful and the homily thought-provoking, as ever. I left feeling at peace with the world – as one should.

That was before the Fall.

Chapter Twenty-one

Monday

Rachel knocked on the studio door which I had left ajar. I called for her to come in, and she entered tentatively. Although she'd been there before, it appeared to intimidate her, but her face brightened when she saw me.

"What a great part of Lon – Sir Nigel! What happened?" she exclaimed, and rushed towards me.

"I broke my ankle."

"How? When? Are you all right? Can you work?"

I burst out laughing.

"Yes, I can work," I said. "Your train fare to London wasn't wasted."

I was sitting on a tall stool near the easel with my leg up on a bentwood chair.

"I'm sorry I can't look after you properly," I said. "You can put your things in there, and the coffee things are set out."

She went into the bedroom and put her coat on the bed with a fashionable paper shopping bag.

"I'm so sorry, do you want to put this off?" she asked, as she moved from the bedroom into the kitchen area and switched on the kettle.

199

"How do you take your coffee?"

"Black, no sugar."

She came to look at me while the kettle boiled.

"What happened?"

"Very dramatic," I said. "I fell off a kerbstone. I thought I was fine until I tried to stand up. I'd just come out of church so there were a lot of people around, many of whom knew me, so I was very lucky.

"I spent the night in hospital and went back to Albany yesterday."

I winced as I adjusted my leg.

"Are you on pain-killers?"

"I didn't think you're too young to want a psychedelic portrait," I said, and she laughed.

"I managed to get down the stairs and out to the courtyard and got a taxi," I said. "It will get easier once I'm used to using a stick."

She made the coffee and handed me a mug.

"Well, this is all new to me," she said, looking at the canvas, onto which I had painted a light burnt umber wash. "Did you start without me?"

"You've heard of 'white coat syndrome'? Well, in the world of artists, there is 'white canvas syndrome.' Putting down a ground colour – it doesn't really matter what – makes the blank canvas less terrifying."

Rachel pondered this.

"After all this time – all those portraits?" she asked.

"I think it's like speaking in public," I replied. "From what my sitters tell me, no matter how experienced they are, they are always terrified – they are just more practised in not letting it show."

While she was considering this, I moved carefully off my stool and grabbed my stick.

"I'm going to need your help in these sittings," I said. "Don't worry, I'll give you a discount."

She laughed.

"What do you need?"

She walked forward to take my arm.

"What I need is for you to take that sketch book and those pencils and give them to me when I sit down over there," I gestured to my armchair. "You may then sit on the sofa – either end, in the middle, I don't mind."

We moved into position (well, I shuffled), Rachel thinking to bring our coffees over.

"Refill those whenever you want," I said.

I picked up the sketch book and a pencil. Opening to a new sheet, I wrote her name and the date.

"Sir Nigel," she began, tentatively, "I don't know how to say this – "

"Don't worry," I said, barely looking up. "You don't want to be painted by moonlight. I've changed my mind, too."

"How – ?"

"Do you know how you *would* like to be painted?"

CR

By lunchtime, we still had not settled on a pose. I now had a good collection of sketches of Rachel's hands, eyes, ears, mouth (open and shut), and head positions in profile, three-quarter and full-face.

She relaxed and we talked of different things, but I asked all my normal questions – repeating some from our first session. "Who was this for?" "Where would it hang?" "Why did she want it painted?"

She considered these questions carefully. Eventually, she replied.

"Since Paul died, I've been very aware that I am alone in the world. Nothing I have will be identified with me for long, even if it's kept."

She fell silent.

"Are you hungry? I saw a Chinese takeaway on the way here. I'll get some."

She was out the door before I could order.

I slowly collected the coffee cups and took them to the kitchen. Moving was slow but not impossible. I got out some cutlery, dishes and bowls, and wondered what I was going to do with Rachel – artistically.

Would she prove to be another of the troubled women I was beginning to think I attracted. There weren't many, but Sophie and Marissa made up for that in the magnitude of their personal problems. (I didn't yet know what had caused Marissa's curious behaviour. I now suspected boredom.) Working with her at the dig, she had been perfectly sensible – and I very much hoped she'd stay that way.

I looked at the drawings I'd done that morning. They'd be useful and had good detail, but a pose hadn't gelled yet. I turned to a fresh page in my sketch book and drew six squares, two across, three down, that nearly filled the sheet. It was a trick taught to me by Julian Beltmore who befriended me in my early days as a painter: rather than draw on an empty sheet of paper, draw the shape of the canvas. The sense of space and placement will give the drawing form and errors of scale, balance and position can be identified and corrected.

I'd see how many possible variations I could sketch before Rachel returned. Very few portraits had figures with both the head and shoulders facing the viewer square-on. Either the body was turned, or the head, and very possibly both, for the classic three-quarter view. Rachel would be easy to paint in any of these positions: it was her surroundings that were the problem.

I drew the one we'd first discussed with her walking towards the viewer, through a garden, with an old brick wall to her left. I drew one of her standing at a window looking out; one of her standing by a pond or stream, looking down at some ducks and coots; one standing contemplating the blank windows of the building at the dig; one of her facing the viewer against a tapestry background in an imitation of Sargent's portrait of Mrs Gardner; and, on a whim, one of her standing in the corner of my studio between my armchair and the sofa. There was the low bookcase, and I imagined my small painting of Sophie on the wall to add balance.

There was a knock on the door and it opened. I had given Rachel my key, and she pushed it open with her body, her hands being full of paper bags.

"I hope you're hungry," she said. "I forgot to ask you what you wanted."

She put her coat in the bedroom and then proceeded to open the containers and place mounds of food on our plates.

"Have you ever used that takeaway?" she asked, digging a fork into some noodles. "They're very nice."

"No, my ruts are very deep, and they don't go that way," I confessed.

"Well, you should," she said, cheerfully. "Where did you learn to use chopsticks?"

I was quiet as I remembered.

"It was on one of the first dates with my late wife," I began. "We'd come to London for a matinée and went to Soho for dinner before heading back to Cambridge.

"Chinese food was one of Vera's favourites. I knew little about it, but that was solved by ordering a dinner for two. The waiter, having placed tea and cups on our empty table, began to set it with a knife and fork, but Vera stopped him, and he put a small pot of chopsticks on the table," I recalled. "I had no idea how to use them but thought I'd better. After all, I was trying to impress this clever lady."

Rachel seemed to like the story, for she had stopped eating and was looking at me, eager for the next bit.

"I watched her and began with something large and simple to lift. After that, she began chatting about reactive resins, and I stopped worrying about the chopsticks with the result that I had no problem," I said. "Now that you've made me think about it, I'll spill everything."

Rachel talked about teaching, how she missed it, but was still feeling "disconnected" following her husband's death.

"Working on the dig was one of the first social things I did," she said. "Coming to London was the first time I'd left Lincolnshire in years."

"Coming for the week must have taken some courage," I said.

"I was ready to begin again just before lockdown, and that set me back," she said. "I was able to do some tutoring online with some former students. That was good for me."

I understood perfectly how and why she'd withdrawn from the world, and also how she now wanted to rejoin it, and do so with enthusiasm.

"Funny how things can come together," she said. "You understand my feelings from your own experience, and the connection with Chief Inspector Warren is a coincidence verging on the weird."

I smiled at her. Men aren't particularly good at empathy, and I could not pretend that what I had felt – as a man – was anything like what she felt as a young lady.

"One of the things the Jesuits taught me was that sometimes God nudges people. It doesn't take away free will, but He presents opportunities which taken can have unexpected results."

"My faith has always been notional," she replied. "In my teens I'd feel devout for a while, but the world would intervene. Weddings, funerals, Christmas and Easter – the usual tick-the-box Anglican."

She stood and collected my plate and took them to the sink.

"Leave them. We have work to do."

She looked at the boxes that still had some food in them.

"Can I put these in the refrigerator?"

"Yes, but then come here and look at these ideas I had while you were out," I said.

For the next forty-five minutes, we talked about the various poses and settings. She listened and considered each of them, made comments yet seemed unenthusiastic about all of them.

We moved to the last one, the frivolous one in the corner of my studio and her reaction was immediately positive.

"I was really just trying to complete six and couldn't think of anything else," I said.

She moved to the corner and looked around.

"Could you make it one of my rooms?" she asked.

"Of course," I said, starting to hobble to my easel.

Rachel began to move out of the corner, but I told her to stay where she was.

"Let's see if we can fix a pose, then I can fill in your things around it and make it yours, which is what it should be," I said, picking up a brush and squirting some colour on my palette.

"I wonder what that says of me, that I like being in a corner?" she mused.

Putting her figure in the corner made the pose emerge naturally. Her body faced the viewer, but her face was turned to near-profile as she contemplated something on the bookshelf. My bookshelf was too low, so I drew it bigger to lift her, so she was only slightly bowed.

"Could you take some books out and put them on the top. . . a few more. . . that's good!" I instructed from the other end of the room. "Now, stand facing me, then turn your head to look at the top book. Now, reach out and put your hand on it.

"Can you hold it like that, please."

I painted for several minutes.

"Is that a comfortable pose?"

"Yes, it's comfortable, but isn't it a bit affected?" she asked.

"You can come see it and decide for yourself."

She came and stood next to me.

"What I suggest is that you go back to Lincolnshire and take pictures of the corner you want to be painted – I can do basic redecoration – and close ups of any objects you might want detailed."

She didn't reply so I turned to look at her. Her eyes were filled with tears.

"You painted me in a long dress," she whispered.

"You may wear whatever you like," I said, uneasily.

"*I have that dress*," she said. "Same neck and waistline, same three-quarter length sleeves."

My rough wasn't that detailed. Rachel was clearly filling in a lot. She silently stared at the image.

"I think we'd better talk," she said. "I bought that dress for a ball that I never had a chance to go to."

Chapter Twenty-two

Monday

By the time I got back to Albany and up the stairs, I was exhausted and in pain. I lay on the sofa (which I am not known to do) and put my leg up on pillows. The cast felt like a cinderblock both in size and weight.

I woke about an hour later to find Sophie setting the table. She approached and put a gin and tonic in my hand.

"Don't worry, you're already a day better," she said.

I was about to chastise her for this Pollyanna attitude when she smiled.

"Cheers," she said.

"And was Lady Marshwood suitably eccentric in rehearsal today?" I asked.

She laughed loudly.

"You always seem to see through me!" she said. "Yes, I 'discovered' that Lady Marshwood was born in Hong Kong. They met while her husband was there on government business. Her ladyship has all the mannerisms – and accent – of a fashionable Hong Kong lady."

I shook my head with amusement.

"And how long was it before Lady Marshwood was back to her traditional self?"

"Two pages," she said, proudly. "It took nearly fifteen minutes because the rest of the cast was laughing so loudly that it took that long to read that far.

"Jason saw the error of his ways and cried, 'I surrender,' to loud applause."

"So, everything's back to normal in *Relative Values* land?" I asked.

"For the moment," Sophie said, with minimal smugness.

I made my way to the table, my movement being more awkward and painful than the trip up the stairs. I managed to sit at the table and lift my leg onto one of the empty chairs.

Sophie had made a simple mixed grill with sausage, bacon, and half a steak for each of us along with some sort of sautéed potatoes and some frozen peas.

"This is very much appreciated," I said. "I am going to have to make some other arrangements until I'm able to get around."

"Yes, the management doesn't like it much when the pizza delivery man shows up. Mason has to tip him."

"I've got a bigger problem than eating," I said. "I've just started Rachel's portrait, and it nearly killed me getting to and from the studio. I'm supposed to be a third through the painting now and I'm already way behind."

I told Sophie about choosing the pose and how everything had gone well until she saw what I'd painted.

"You really do attract them," she said, without much sympathy. "Did you take her in your arms and offer your shoulder to cry on?"

"I would have run out the door had I been able to," I said.

"That wouldn't have been nice," she said, coldly. "What did you say?"

"I told her to go back to Lincolnshire and photograph the room we decided to place her in and come back next week with whatever she wanted to wear," I said. "However, on the way up the stairs, it occurred to me that she might enjoy some detective work, too."

Sophie was intrigued by this idea.

"What sort of detective work? Skulking around the dig and trampling evidence?"

"No, tracking down Max and Marissa and finding out all she can about Bickering Hall and Priory – the village, too, if there actually was one."

"You've got an idea?"

"Not a particularly good one, but just a suspicion that there is a link between the Hall and the paintings," I said. "And, if there is, we might learn more about the ruin we've been digging."

Sophie leaned forward with interest.

"Also," I continued, "she knows Detective Inspector Covell and might be able to get some information from him about the pistol and the body."

"Do you have her mobile number?" Sophie asked, then muttered, sotto voce, "Stupid question. Call when we've finished and get her to come here in the morning and give her instructions. That could be interesting; I wish I could be here."

We finished the meal talking about Sophie's rehearsal and how I'd manage the rest of the week.

"You'll just have to arrange regular deliveries from F&M," Sophie said.

It didn't sound like it, but she was joking. Comfortable though we were, a weekly delivery from Fortnum & Mason was not for us. I wouldn't starve, though.

Sophie retrieved my mobile phone and put it on the table.

"I'll call when we finish," I said.

"No, do it before it gets too late. Even Rachel has a life beyond sitting for you."

I called the number while Sophie began washing the dishes and making coffee.

"Rachel. This is Nigel Thomas. I'm not interrupting anything, am I?"

I wasn't, and I arranged for her to come to my set in the morning.

When Sophie came in with the coffee, it was clear she was trying to suppress laughter.

"What?" I demanded. "Is my whole life a source of amusement to you?"

"This is Sir Nigel Paintbrush, you may remember me from today when you spent five hours in my company," she mimicked. "Could you come to my rooms at Albany tomorrow? I have a proposition for you."

She laughed flamboyantly.

"What girl could refuse such an offer?" she asked, still laughing.

"I didn't say that," I protested.

"The bit about the proposition, you did, I'm afraid."

"Should I call her back and apologise?"

"What is it with you and telephones. You just can't wait to get off them," Sophie said, with a condescension usually associated with sick children. "Anyway, why call her back? She responded favourably to your solicitation."

"Good night, Sophie," I said. "Thank you for your thoughtful supper."

There was no point in saying anything more. She kissed the top of my head and prepared to go.

"Do you need anything else?"

"Just a few bottles of painkillers. I'll get them on the way to bed."

"'Noted Painter Dies of Overdose'," she mused. "That should jack up the value of your pictures nicely."

She waved her arm around the room.

"Do I inherit all of these, too? If so, I might be able to afford weekly deliveries from Fortnum's."

She waved and left.

೩

Even with the gin and tonic, wine and painkillers, it still took several hours to fall asleep. After the first hour, I turned on the light and read until I was awakened by the book hitting the floor, and I turned out the light.

While I wasn't comfortable in the morning, at least the pain wasn't as bad. Sophie came in before going to rehearsal to see if she were an heiress.

"Sorry to disappoint you," I said. "I'm still alive."

She smiled. Gone was the flirtatious tease. Her concern was genuine, and I appreciated it.

"I hope your meeting goes well today," she said. "I'll give April a call this evening to see if there is any news on the skeleton."

She looked at the untidiness on my dining room table.

"Will you be working on the watercolours here?"

"What else would I do after you and Rachel leave?"

"I don't know. Say a rosary?"

"Have a good rehearsal, Miss Gordon."

೩

Rachel arrived at ten-thirty as arranged. Sophie had left my door on latch and Mason had directed her to my set.

She tapped tentatively on my door.

"Sir Nigel?"

I welcomed her and told her to put her coat in my small study. I was standing uneasily at my armchair and sat down as soon as she closed the door.

"There's hardly a square foot of space without a picture on it!" she exclaimed, looking around. "How many of them are yours?"

"Only two. Most of the others are done by friends," I said. "Have a nose around I don't think there's anything incriminating in sight. Besides, I'm apt to ask you to get something."

"Oh!" she said, surprised, when she saw the painting of Vera above the fireplace.

"My first portrait," I said. "I had the audacity of youth to submit it to the Summer Exhibition, and it was accepted. It was never for sale, but I got three commissions on the back of it, and less than a decade later was made a Fellow of the R.A. Not bad for a Royal Navy dropout."

Rachel laughed easily. She seemed more at home here than she did at the studio.

"Well, I am going to be audacious, too," she said. "May I make you – and myself – a cup of coffee?"

I smiled at her. She had a naturally ordinary manner. She wasn't being coy, bold, flirtatious or even cheeky; she was simply being practical.

"I thought you'd never ask."

I had left the mugs, cafetière and sugar out, so it wouldn't take her long.

"Sophie told me that my invitation to you to come here could have been construed as suggestive. I am sorry if you misunderstood me."

She giggled.

She giggled rather than laughed. I wasn't certain why, but it had a distinct charm. Later, while painting her, I asked why she didn't laugh.

"When you begin teaching, the advice is don't smile until at least Easter," she said. "In May, you might venture a feeble joke. After that, you might smile and chuckle, but laughing is discouraged. It seems I've kept the habit. Would you like me to be more demonstrative in my joviality?"

She gave me the mug and sat in the corner of the sofa nearest me.

"I won't take much of your time," I began. "Here is a page of sketches of the angles of the room that would be most helpful. Also, if you could scribble on these drawings where the light comes from, that would be useful, too. I will probably paint it as though the light was from a higher source than your windows are apt to be, but at least the room will still look familiar to you."

She took the page and looked at it.

"I could never scribble on these," she said.

"Rachel, I don't do anything more special than your work as a teacher. How many of the things you have written have you thrown away? Don't attach special significance to life's detritus."

She didn't reply, nor, I think, did she pay any attention to what I had said. She held the drawings as if not knowing what to do with them, so I held out my hand, and she gave them back to me.

Her mouth opened when I folded it into a size that would fit into her handbag and gave them.

"Now, apart from collecting some photos of the space you wish to be painted in, I wondered if you might be willing to undertake some research for me. I have no idea how you usually fill your days, but if you had time to do this for me, I think you'd find it interesting, and it might help solve some of the mysteries of Bickering."

○ʒ

Rachel was immediately agreeable. She took out a notebook and, in the next hour, filled a dozen or so pages with questions, notes, suggestions, hypotheses and suspicions.

And now, for a while, the narrative is hers.

Part Two

Chapter Twenty-three

Tuesday

Rachel's Notebook

There is something very strange going on. The meeting with Ligeia Gordon, the finding of the buried pistol parts, the decision to request my portrait to be painted, and the completely unpredictable coincidence of Ligeia and Sir Nigel knowing Chief Inspector Warren have caught me off balance. If I thought about it too much, it would frighten me.

Sophie is very nice. I didn't realise who she was until she'd been there a few days. Her trained voice rang a bell, but she was just so – *ordinary* – and no more interesting than the others, that I still find it hard to believe.

There is some mystery there with her, but I have no idea what it is. Are she and Sir Nigel lovers? Something is holding them together though he's a lot older than she is. I know that shouldn't make a difference these days, but somehow their affection is more *verbal* than physical. I wonder which can't or won't do it.

Sir Nigel is a methodical thinker – and he seems to have read far more than I have – though he has the advantage of being twice my age.

He has given me two weeks to complete my tasks. Some of them are fairly simple – talking to April and Marissa about what they know about the paintings, any stories about Bickering Hall they might have heard, and anything they know about the family that had owned it.

He also asked if I could track down old maps of the area around Bickering. I suggested I start with the parish records – if any – and then try Horncastle before going to Lincoln.

Next, he asked if I could contact Max Hillyard and see if he could help fill in some gaps about the history of Bickering Hall, Bickering Priory, Bickering Place and the ruined building.

I began with my main task which was to photograph the room where I wanted to be painted.

A teacher and a young policeman don't earn a lot of money, but with some savings and luck, we found the cottage in Bardney. Built facing the Witham near Bardney Lock, there was a row of four small houses. The story is that these were built for workers at a landing stage, for loading and unloading barges. Three of the houses remain and Paul and I managed to get the one standing on its own.

It needed complete renovation, and we camped in it as we did it. I don't know how; I was marking papers and preparing lessons, and Paul was working all sorts of hours and continuing his training, too.

While there are still things that we planned to do, the house was finished and decorated by the time Paul was killed. I have done nothing since except keep it clean and as it was.

It would have been small for a family house, but for two it was comfortable, and for one, it's spacious.

The room and corner to feature in the painting was obvious, but I spent a day moving furniture to compose the picture I wanted.

I didn't want a fussy painting, but I wanted it to look elegant. I've never been a glamour girl, but I wanted to look like someone worth painting, and I wanted a record of wearing The Dress.

As you might imagine, Paul and I had little time for a social life. Still, Bardney is very small, and we came to know people through the church, the pub and the odd connection with the school or the force. There was the odd school friend, like Marissa, who was still in the area and available to meet for the occasional lunch or supper, but other old friends were married with children (several of whom I taught) or moved away.

Having no brothers or sisters, I was used to being on my own so didn't crave company the way others did. I had a pretty good idea of what being married to someone in the police would be, that there would be nights alone, awkward assignments, and much that Paul couldn't share with me, but we were happy with our jobs and with each other.

If I had to guard against anything in my work for Sir Nigel, it would be to keep my reports short but complete, and not try to interpret anything. English Literature specialists will interpret shopping lists: look for alliteration, rhythms and hidden rhymes, not to mention character analysis and "deeper meanings."

But I was telling you about The Dress.

We were invited to a formal party at one of the old hotels in Lincoln. One of the top officers was retiring or celebrating a major birthday or wedding anniversary and Paul wanted me to go. He would have been one of the lowest ranking people there as well as one of the youngest, and the whole idea of it filled me with dread.

I made a deal with him that I'd go and never say another word of complaint if he bought me a nice dress. He offered to come with me to buy it. He was with his duty at Scotland Yard and the idea of shopping in London was very attractive.

On Friday night, I went down to meet him. We had a romantic dinner, a late night walk through London and a late morning before we went shopping.

Paul knew instinctively how to treat me: let me choose and only offered an opinion when asked. The party was in the early summer, and I suspected that the old dears who were the wives of the brass would probably wear black.

I chose a yellow satin dress. The saleslady called it "butter yellow" but I just thought of it as "summer yellow." It was a good, strong solid colour, solidly yellow, not veering towards lime, or the paleness of lemon, or the richer gold of butterscotch.

It was three quarter-length with three-quarter sleeves and a square neckline, so no one could accuse me of being immodest. All they'd be able to say was that I was yellow.

Rereading this, I am reminded of a D H Lawrence story where he goes on and on, naming things that are yellow from the sun to the girl's hair, the flowers – I hate Lawrence.

I took the dress back to Lincolnshire and hung it in the bedroom and looked at it when I was lying in bed and admired it when it caught the sun in the morning.

Before I put it in the cupboard, I received the news that Paul had been killed. The dress went into a black hanging garment bag with a handful of mothballs and cedar chips where it's been for six years.

This is the first time I've ever been tempted to look at it again. It might be full of moth holes, or worse, hideously out of fashion.

∽

I delayed taking the bag from the cupboard for two days, and I hadn't started any of the other jobs for Sir Nigel either.

On impulse, I drove to Bickering Place. I slowed down as I passed the site but there was no activity. There was only a small stretch where I could see the ruin before the bramble-covered hill, but the police tape was gone and no one was there.

I drew up in front of Bickering Place and was getting out of the car when the front door opened, and April came out.

"I wondered who that could have been, Rachel!" she said, welcoming me.

"You're not expecting visitors, are you?" I asked.

"I thought it might have been Marissa. She said she'd be back in time for coffee," she replied. "Come in and I'll find another mug.

"I miss having the crowd around for lunches," she said, walking into the house.

"It must have been a lot of work."

"What else have I got to do. It was either that or the garden."

We went into the kitchen, and she pulled out a chair for me and began making coffee.

"Have you come to see Marissa?" she asked.

It was a curious question, but that was April.

"I wanted to see you both," I said. "I wanted to see if anything new was happening at the dig, and Sir Nigel asked if I'd do a few things for him."

April had just put a plate of her gingerbread on the table when I heard a car on the gravel drive.

"That will be Marissa," April said, wiping her hands on her apron. "I'll get the door for her."

I knew Bickering Place was now Marissa's house, but the way April was acting like a Mrs Hudson or Mrs Pierce seemed unnecessary.

"Rachel!" Marissa exclaimed, entering the kitchen. "Come to relieve our solitude?"

Brushing aside that it was I who had lived in solitude for years without a visit from her, I replied:

"I am on a mission," I declared. "Sir Nigel has asked me to do some research for him."

"He should have come himself," April said. "He knows he's always welcome here. He and Marissa get on so well."

I had been warned about that delusion.

"Sir Nigel is unable to come, which is why I am here," I began. "He has broken his ankle and has retreated to his Albany set."

"How did you find out?" Marissa asked as neutrally as she could. "Did he call you?"

Something made me hold back on telling them about the portrait.

"I was in London for a few days. Sir Nigel, Sophie and I met for lunch," I told them. "I discovered that they knew the chief inspector who was wounded when Paul was killed."

That was enough to quell their curiosity.

"Sir Nigel fell off the pavement a day later and called me up to tell me," I said, but they were still focused on the coincidence with Detective Chief Inspector Warren.

"Small world," April said, absently.

"And talking of guns, have you learned anything new about the skeleton?"

Marissa appeared annoyed by the whole thing, and over the course of coffee, lunch and a walk around the garden, it all came out.

"The skeleton pre-dates the pistol," Marissa explained. "There's no obvious cause of death. The theory is that someone – we'll probably never know who – took shelter or hid there and died.

"The bones showed signs of animal teeth marks which also explains the way they are scattered," Marissa explained. "However, there are no bullet marks, blunt instrument damage, sword cuts or mace fractures."

"Do they have any idea how old it is?" I asked.

Marissa and April glanced at each other. I wasn't sure whether it was that the subject simply made them uncomfortable – hearing about real crimes from Paul had made me immune to discussing corpses – or something else, I couldn't tell.

"Whatever that building was appears to have fallen out of use in the early eighteenth century," Marissa said. "Detective Inspector Covell thinks the skeleton is from sometime between then and 1800.

"No one wants to spend time or money on carbon dating or DNA," she added, bitterly.

I moved away from that topic to give them a chance to recover so I didn't sound like I was interrogating them.

"Oh!" I said, "I forgot to give you a message from Sir Nigel. He says he's working on your watercolours and sketches, and that his inability to walk hasn't rendered him completely useless."

April smiled.

"He's working from Albany, but he's not bed-bound," I said.

"You've been there?" Marissa asked, again, in a voice calculatedly devoid of implication.

I decided to come clean.

"I should have told you: he's painting my portrait," I said, but continued quickly to prevent comment. "I had two sittings in Southwark, but then he broke his ankle over the weekend. I went to Albany because I hadn't been able to make up my mind about a pose, what to wear or anything like that.

"Basically, he sent me away to get organised, but he also asked my help with the research," I said.

I could see Marissa about to make a comment that wasn't neutral, but April spoke first.

"How wonderful to get your picture painted!" she said. "Marissa loved working with Nigel, didn't you."

Far from meeting my eye with a challenging look, Marissa looked demure and even blushed.

I thought this was a good time to move the conversation on.

"One of the other things he asked me to look into was the history of Bickering, hall, priory and place."

Chapter Twenty-four

Tuesday
Rachel's Notebook

Asking April and Marissa about Bickering felt like an invasion of their privacy since the Gilliat family had lived there for more than two centuries. Marissa was the last of the direct line and if she didn't have a child soon, that would be the end completely.

Growing up, Bickering Place was their family home. Each generation had done something to the house or garden, and they had continued to farm the land. Remarkably little of it had been sold off.

Questioning them was even more awkward because Sir Nigel hadn't told me exactly what he wanted to know, let alone why. I mean, I could guess that it was related to the paintings and maybe to the dig site, but was he using me to delve into Marissa's past in some post-modernist way?

Still, there was something in the way Marissa seemed to react whenever Sir Nigel was mentioned. April was obviously very fond of him, but Marissa was more ambiguous.

I shouldn't be surprised because the relationship between him and Sophie has me completely baffled. I've puzzled that one since I met them. They appear to be flirtatious friends but nothing more, yet they are also closer than many couples I know.

It makes Paul and me look positively dull in our simple and obvious adoration of each other.

઼

That was getting morbid. The waves of loss aren't violent – they don't need to be – they arrive like a warm swell and simply drown me. It doesn't happen often or for as long anymore, but, for me at least, it's like stepping off the planet for a while. I go through the motions, do what work I have and try to act normal.

I know that people think, "It's been six years now, so she must be fine." To tell them any different would only invite suggestions of "getting away," meeting new people, or counselling.

Of course, it is six years, and the bad days are few, but no less intense. I feel comfortable and safe in my house – our home – and the place itself doesn't bring sadness, only good memories.

With that awareness of the sense of place, I began asking about Bickering. At first, my questions were general and to both April and Marissa.

What did they know of the village? When did it disappear? What family built and owned the hall? Were there significant subsequent owners? When and why was it torn down? [Sir Nigel asked me not to mention "fire" so as not to suggest answers.]

I didn't fully understand the mention of a fire and presumed that one of the paintings Sir Nigel was researching depicted a blaze.

He also suggested I ask a few questions about the priory. It had been small, disreputable and, like the priory in nearby Minting, it had been remotely run by several orders until the dissolution. The Abbey of Bardney, a few hundred yards from me, had had a troubled history due to meddlesome kings and others but was much bigger and more respected than these smaller houses.

This is what I learned (or didn't). April and Marissa seemed to share the same stories as there was little debate between them in their narrative.

1.   Bickering was only ever a common description of the area around the hall and the priory. It was never a proper village, though there were cottages and houses around the area for servants, farmworkers, craftsmen and pilgrims.

2.   They didn't know of any connection between Bickering and Beckering or Holton cum Beckering some eight miles away.

3.   The hall stood several hundred yards east of the priory on the north side of the existing road. (The later building at the dig was on the south side of the road, more or less across from the priory.)

4.   Neither knew anything about the building at the excavation apart from what was talked about during the dig: c. seventeenth century, built with Tudor brick and some stone, presumably from Bickering Hall or the priory. They believed it had been used as a barn or animal enclosure since the mid-eighteenth century. Marissa said some of the trees cut from within the building were at least a hundred years old. Maybe as much as a hundred fifty.

5.   Neither knew exactly where the gothic window now in Bickering Place was found. Marissa thought it was from the field on the south side of the road, April that it was found between the priory and the hall.

By the time I had dragged this out of them, I felt I had outstayed my welcome, and I had not mentioned the paintings. I gathered that Marissa didn't know anything about them, so I would have to speak to April again.

Marissa did say that she had copies of the odd old map that she would duplicate for me, but Max was the one to contact in that department; his preparations had been more extensive than hers.

"I focused on getting the team together, the tools, the food and accommodation and day to day operations," she said. "Max was more strategic. He told me what he wanted to do, and I'd allocate the manpower."

I thanked them and got up to leave. The telephone rang as I reached the front door and Marissa went to answer it.

"Sir Nigel asked if I could talk to you about the paintings, too," I said. "I understand Marissa doesn't know anything."

That sounds harsh when written down, but April understood what I meant.

"Of course. Come for tea around four tomorrow," April said. "Marissa is in Cambridge for the day seeing some old friends."

"Max? – I only ask because I need to contact him, too, and don't want to bother him if he's tied up."

April gave a sad smile.

"Poor Max. Such a nice chap and adores Marissa," she said. "Never mind, Nigel's still available."

[I wrote this in my report to Sir Nigel without comment, but once again, I wondered what was going on in his – and Marissa's – life.]

In the early evening, I telephoned Max. He was in East Sussex doing an excavation, but he didn't tell me where or what. He'd be returning to Lincoln at the weekend, and we arranged to meet for a pub lunch. He suggested The Carpenters at Fiskerton which was conveniently between us.

He was surprised to hear from me and seemed disappointed when I told him it was really a professional call, not a social one. I was surprised as I had the impression that Marissa was his Dulcinea. Luckily, he still sounded enthusiastic to talk about the Bickering site, though he cannot have listed it as one of his successes.

In the evening, I typed a summary of the above and emailed it to Sir Nigel and hoped he'd be pleased with my efforts.

ℭ

Wednesday

Rachel's Notebook

I had hoped for a reply from Sir Nigel, but being old, his life doesn't centre on his smartphone. Anyway, he'd be working his way through the paintings for Marissa. (I'd love to know what she paid for a dozen specially commissioned paintings, plus his travel, room and board. Probably considerably more than I was paying for my portrait, which reminds me, he did promise me a discount and expenses. Must record my mileage.)

By lunchtime I had done my usual Wednesday chores (no, I'm not OCD – I don't think – but as a teacher, I lived by timetables, and it seemed a good way to run our home as well. I don't think Paul ever caught on to the fact that I did certain jobs on certain days).

After lunch and before going to see April, I had decided to unzip the black bag and look at The Dress. I knew there was a chance that I would no longer like it, or that it would be too painful to wear, or – worst of all – that it wouldn't fit.

Knowing it would stink of mothballs, I took it outside and hung it on the clothesline, held my breath, pulled down the zipper and peeled back the black cover.

My memory of the colour was exact, as was that of the details of the style. What I had forgotten was how beautifully made it was. Age had done nothing to wither it and, checking the seams, the stitching was fine and, in many places, invisible.

It did pong of camphor, though. I left it hanging in the breeze and would bring it in before leaving for Bickering Place.

I felt proud of myself as I watched it sway with the wind from inside before I noticed the tears on my cheeks.

☙

April welcomed me when I went back to Bickering Place. She had set out an assortment of small squares of gingerbread, shortbread and bread pudding on the kitchen table. I wondered about ever fitting into my yellow dress.

We chatted briefly about general things, then focused on the dig before I moved to the paintings.

"I haven't seen the paintings," I began. "I understand that Sir Nigel has had them cleaned and revarnished, but not restored."

"He hasn't varnished Marissa's portrait yet," April said, throwing me off. "Maybe he'll do it when he comes back."

Sir Nigel had a number of reasons to come back to Bickering Place, but I suspected he'd use his ankle to send Sophie, but that didn't solve the problem of the varnishing.

"From what I understand, there is a portrait, a flower painting and a landscape," I said. "The first two are very old, he thinks."

"I've lived here for forty years," April began. "I've only seen the pictures a few times when we've had work done or redecorated and had to move things. No one ever liked them. The portrait was burned, the flower painting very dark, and the landscape rather uninteresting and not fit to look at."

She thought for a moment.

"That's what Titus and Marissa said, at least," she added. "I was never interested enough to look at them in any detail."

Sir Nigel had warned me about April's gingerbread, and I found myself picking up a third small square.

"Do you know of any connection of the paintings with Bickering Hall?"

"Not really," April said. "Titus would have been the one to ask. It was his family's house, not mine. All I know is that this house dates to the fifteenth century and that it was rebuilt in Tudor times, in the reign of Queen Elizabeth. Then it was rebuilt again. I've always assumed – and Titus never said otherwise – that the pictures were always here. I also gathered that they had been in the cupboard while he was growing up."

"Do you know why?"

April gave a condescending smile.

"Well, I expect for the same reasons we left them there: we didn't like them."

Chapter Twenty-five

Thursday

J received emails daily from Rachel regarding her progress. She felt she was accomplishing very little, yet she was confirming my suspicions. All I needed was corroborative evidence.

I received a call late Wednesday from Helena Stirakis who asked if I could come to the Courtauld on Friday to meet with a few people – she was curiously unspecific – and collect the paintings.

She seemed genuinely solicitous when I told her about my impaired mobility, but she was still eager that I come if I could.

"We'll look after the pictures until you're able to collect them, but there are a few things I think you'll find interesting," she said.

Curators have a language of noncommittal words and phrases that rivals that of politicians. There are dozens of words used to hedge their bets and evade definite statements. As a modern artist – unlikely to be faked – who signs all his paintings on the front and back, I can afford to be contemptuous of these practices.

The other reason I am contemptuous is that this circumlocution is seldom about art but only about money, preserving all possible value while avoiding being sued.

Nevertheless, that money affords livelihoods for some truly amazing people with an expertise that I envy and admire. That they are ultimately in the pay of those who want the "right" answers does not compromise their dedication and knowledge.

Needless to say, these are opinions I tend to keep to myself. But not always.

My ankle was hurting much less when I limped from the taxi into the Courtauld early Friday afternoon and took the freight lift to the studio where Marissa's paintings were.

I was surprised to see two flower paintings on easels as well as another portrait similar in style to Marissa's. There was also another woman standing near the pictures.

Helena greeted me and offered me her arm as I stepped from the lift. There was a tactical advantage in letting her think I was more infirm than I was. How I might use it, I didn't know.

She led me to a high stool facing both flower pictures.

"Sir Nigel, this is Dr Meadow Mannering, of Birkbeck College," Dr Stirakis said. "Dr Mannering is a botanist."

She held out her hand, which I took.

"Do they still have botanists?" I asked. "I thought they were all biochemists, bioengineers and such."

"There are a few of us left," she said, cheerfully.

As I suspected with a name like Meadow, she was American.

"You won't believe this, Nigel," Helena began, "but even though I only have a few square feet in a London suburb, I am a keen gardener. I met Meadow when she gave a garden club lecture in Greenwich.

"When I suspected some – shall we say – problems – with this picture, I called her in to have a look," she explained.

"Problems" wasn't a word commonly used by anyone today. Things are "challenges," so I knew something serious was up.

"I'm going to do something I don't usually do, Sir Nigel," Helena continued. "Once Meadow and I have related our various findings, I am going to suggest a scenario – I know you like positing them – and these paintings are so suggestive, that I think I need to express them."

She gave me a conspiratorial look.

"But not for quoting or for publication," I said.

"I knew you'd understand."

"And you, Dr Mannering?"

She laughed.

"I have no reputation in the art world to risk," she said, easily. "I doubt what I tell you is worth quoting but you are welcome to."

After a little more chat, Helena began her findings.

"Sir Nigel, I am sure you will know – or have suspected – most of what I am going to tell you, but this will confirm your own conclusions.

We moved to the floral picture.

"The picture is in very good condition for its age. It has not, as you noted, been relined, nor is there any sign of major restoration. There is the odd place – particularly in the background – where some paint loss has been filled in. There are only a few areas, and this retouching appears to have been done in the eighteenth century."

If restoration had been done that long ago, presumably, it still would have been hanging somewhere. I made a mental note to relate this to Marissa.

"The picture is very early for a flower painting of this type," Helena continued. "We've done some pigment analysis and can narrow the timeframe suggested by James Beech to 1580 to 1610. There is a paint and canvas analysis in the report. I can give details, but it's Meadow who has the most interesting insights."

This was unlike Helena to handover the big story, and I was intrigued.

Meadow had a blend of American confidence and British academic reticence about her which made an interesting contrast.

"Helena called me in to have a look at some of the flowers here that she didn't immediately recognise," she began. "I am sure you will recognise the lilies and roses, and there are summer phlox, hawthorns, foxgloves, lavender, bachelor's buttons, butter cups, and yellow irises."

She pointed to each as she named them.

"These are relatively well known and common, either as painted, or in some more modern variation," she said. "Now, here are the interesting ones: this is a form of gentian that would have only been found in the UK at that time. The same is true of this western ramping fumitory which was only found in Cornwall, and this variety of Hawkweed is only found in the UK."

I tried to take in the words and images, but this was a subject I knew nearly nothing about, except for some of the symbolism.

"Do you see where this is going?" Helena asked.

"I think I'm beginning to."

"I had my first suspicion when I saw the ladybird down here," Helena said, pointing to the small red insect. "As it happens, Meadow is a Roman Catholic like you, and although I am not practicing, the Greek Orthodox Church has similar traditions."

I looked from Helena to Meadow for an explanation.

"Go ahead, Meadow. This is your field," Helena said.

"I am sure you know what the roses and lilies suggest, but all of the other flowers are associated with the Virgin Mary, too – apart from those that were uniquely English.

"What we have is a floral testament to the Catholic faith in this late Tudor painting," she said. "Helena had to explain the ladybird to me. In America, we call them ladybugs, and everyone associates the Blessed Virgin with blue, not red – but Helena tells me that red was Mary's colour until late mediaeval times, and that they were known as 'Our Lady's Birds.'"

I was glad I was sitting down. Virtually no religious art from the pre-Tudor period survived. The Great Iconoclasm had destroyed nearly all of it.

"This is hugely exciting, unique and exceptional," Helena said, unable to restrain her enthusiasm.

"I've never seen anything like this," I said.

"I haven't either," Helena agreed. "More tests and analysis need to be done, but if it's real – and I cannot see any reason at this time why it isn't – it is one of the major discoveries of English art since – well, *ever*!"

I looked at both of them. Meadow clearly had no idea of the significance of what she'd helped to discover but was looking pleased.

"Unmistakably English. Unmistakably late Tudor. Unmistakably Roman Catholic," Helena proclaimed. "This is going to create quite a stir."

We sat in awe of the painting, its presumed history and its significance.

After a while, I said:

"This dovetails with the portrait, doesn't it?" I asked.

246

Helena nodded, trying again to control her excitement.

"Again, Beech's estimate was on the money," she said. "He said 1525 to 1575. I'd put it between 1525 and 1535, give or take five years. We can do dendrochronology on the panel to confirm.

"I don't think you said, but the likelihood is that these two pictures came from the same place," she said. "That would give us a Plantagenet-supporting Catholic family."

Meadow looked puzzled.

"The white boar emblem on the choker," I said. "That was Richard III's badge."

Meadow uttered an expletive common in both the United States and Britain, then quickly apologised.

"It fits," Helena said.

"Where's it from?" Meadow asked.

"A house with fifteenth century roots in Lincolnshire," I said. "They've been in a closet for centuries."

"Probably out of habit," Helena said. "It would have been at least potentially dangerous to have them on show until the mid-seventeen hundreds."

"Are they still with a Catholic family?" Meadow asked.

"No. The current family bought the house in the seventeen hundreds," I said. "The connection I'm trying to make is between an old hall that was nearby and the smaller residence."

Helena took a deep breath.

"And that fits with my scenario," she said. "Both of these are paintings that reflect affluence. The smoke and fire damage suggests they were in the same building, most likely a large house or hall. The subject matter suggests, as we've mentioned, that this was a pro-Plantagenet Catholic family.

"Following the fire – or deliberate destruction of the house – these were rescued and hidden, possibly in a new residence. Their survival also suggests that members of the family survived."

I nodded.

"There was a small priory very near where the old house is supposed to have been," I said.

Helena smiled with satisfaction.

"The secret code of the flowers will not have been recognised after a few generations," she continued. "By then, it may simply have been unfashionable."

"This all fits," Meadow interrupted. "The flowers were given Protestant names – the names that are used today: Spiderwort was Our Lady's Tears but is commonly known now as Wandering Jew – though that's not politically correct. Summer phlox was Christ's Cross, Baby's Breath was Our Lady's Veil, Bachelor's Buttons were Mary's Crown – and so on.

"Each of these," she indicated the flowers in the painting, "had a Catholic name, but as Helena has said, these would have been forgotten in a few generations."

Meadow moved to the other flower painting.

"You probably wondered why this was here," she said, smiling. "Helena brought it up for me so that I could show you something else. The flowers on this other one are all in bloom at the same time. The Catholic flowers, flower at different times, so you could never have them all together like this. That shows a deliberate selection and secret message."

"As survivors of the Great Iconoclasm, these are amazing," Helena said. Then added, "Assuming they are not like the sophisticated fakes you showed me the last time."

Meadow looked up.

"Another, long story," I said. "To the best of my knowledge, what I have told you is true."

"What you will need to do is establish a link between the old house and where these were found," she said.

"I have someone working on that now."

We stared some more at the two pictures, trying to imagine the world they came from, the overturning of five hundred years of life and the burial of their truth.

"And the final painting?" I asked. My leg was starting to hurt and while I could have spent hours more talking to Helena and Meadow, picking their brains and debating possible historical situations, what I wanted was to get home, swallow some drugs and have a nap.

"I don't think I need to tell you much about this one," Helena said. "It's probably by an amateur local painter, but local to where, I have no idea. The land is flat which could be Lincolnshire, but just as easily Essex, Suffolk, Cambridge or half a dozen other counties.

"A date of 1780 to 1830 would be the range," she said. "It's not badly painted. The composition is a little unbalanced, but the perspective is good and the colours tone well, even if they are a little unsubtle."

"I told Alicia that it looked like something that hung in a local pub," I said. "She replied that there were enough food and drink stains to come to that conclusion, not to mention the nicotine and soot."

Helena laughed.

"It was good to have her swabs," she said. "We tested them after testing the painting and they supported our conclusions."

She handed me two thick documents and a large envelope.

"These will tell you everything the two of us could find out," Helena said. "The rest is up to you."

Chapter Twenty-six

Saturday

Rachel's Notebook

Given the meagreness of the information about the history of the paintings that I was able to send to Sir Nigel, his response was very appreciative. I mentioned to him that I would be seeing Max Hillyard today and he asked me to find out about the family that owned Bickering Hall, like were they supporters of the Tudors? What that has to do with the paintings, I don't know, but if that's what he wants.

After airing The Dress, I hung it in my bedroom so I could look at it. I haven't dared to try it on yet and hope I can still fit into it without it looking like it was painted on.

As I got ready to go to The Carpenters, it struck me that this was the first time I'd have gone out on my own to meet a man for a meal since Paul died. I'd been out, of course, but they'd been parties and groups of people meeting up for a drink or a meal, not a one-to-one date.

I told myself this wasn't a date but a business meeting and that thought managed to get me to stop crying. If I kept that in mind, I could enjoy my lunch without feeling guilty.

I got to the pub with ten minutes to spare and went in, was shown to our table, ordered a soft drink. I took out my notebook; I had to look and feel business-like otherwise my self-deception would not succeed.

While I waited, I assessed what I knew about Max. It wasn't much. I knew he'd met Marissa in Cambridge when they were doing the same course. I also knew that he was – according to Marissa and April – smitten with her and had been carrying a torch since then.

At the dig, they appeared to work professionally together, debating strategies, priorities, and laughing. I saw no uneasiness between them, nor any overt displays of anything but the level of public affection of people who had known each other for two decades.

If he were pining for Marissa, Max hid it pretty well – at least from me.

I was absorbed in my notes when I heard a voice.

"I'm sorry if I kept you waiting," Max said, with an ease that suggested he said it may times. "I – um – well, you know."

"I haven't been here that long," I said, indicating my barely touched drink.

He sat down.

"Good choice to meet here," he said. "I haven't been here for a while."

"Nor have I," I said. "On days I wasn't at school, I used to meet Paul here. As a matter of fact, I haven't been here since he died."

"I'm sorry," Max said. "Do you want to eat somewhere else?"

I had suggested meeting here, so I couldn't go soppy.

"It's taken me a long time, but recently I've tried to get out more," I said.

He looked at me, waiting for me to continue. When I didn't, he picked up the menu.

"I'm sorry, Max," I said. "As I said on the telephone, Sir Nigel has asked me to gather some information for him. He was particularly interested in the history of the priory and Bickering Hall, and if there ever actually was a village known as Bickering. Oh, yes. He also wanted to know about the family or families that owned the hall."

He gave me a big smile. It was not the reaction I was expecting.

"You can stop hiding, Rachel," he said, gently. "I'll tell you what I know. I brought some copies of maps you can send Sir Nigel, but you don't need to play the academic researcher, investigative journalist with me.

"We've not been friends, but we've been on the edges of each other's lives for twenty years."

His manner so easy and natural. He wasn't posing, he wasn't acting stupid, scolding or possessive.

I fell silent and looked down. I might have felt scolded, but didn't, rather, it was if he was turning on the lights again or opening a window.

"Are you ready to order?" a voice said next to me.

"I'm ready," said Max. "Are you?"

I'd been there fifteen minutes and Max had hardly glanced at the menu but gave his order.

I scanned the menu with the desperation one does in such circumstances and latched on to something that I thought I'd have a hope of enjoying.

When the waiter left, Max began to answer my questions and made no further reference to his comments about me playing the great detective.

"What's Sir Nigel's interest in Bickering Hall and priory?" he asked. "He doesn't need to know any of this for his paintings, does he?"

I shook my head.

"No. Marissa gave him some old paintings – I haven't seen them – I can only think his questions relate to them.

"Have the police turned the site back over to Marissa?" I asked, suddenly realising that I hadn't asked about it.

"Yes. They're done," Max said. "What they haven't done is returned the finds."

"And the skeleton?"

"Still waiting on results," he said. "Not murdered, it appears – unless he was run through with a rapier or dagger that didn't nick any bones."

"And the building? I think Sir Nigel has a theory on that," I said.

"Yes, he told me on the first day he was at the dig," Max said. "I've tried to forget it so I can keep an open mind. Did he tell you?"

"No," I said. "Sophie was the one who said he'd had an idea."

"That's good," Max said. "I asked him to keep it to himself for the time being."

"Do you think his guess is right?"

"That would be telling," Max said, with a cheeky smile. "Let's say, I'm still considering it."

He stopped, then grew more serious.

"As for the other questions," he began. "It's all tied up with politics and religion. Lincolnshire was a really soupy mess in the sixteenth and seventeenth centuries."

As he spoke, I had a good look at him. He had strong features, bright, intelligent blue eyes, and a pleasing voice with an edge of Lincolnshire to it. While many considered him rather effete, he had demonstrated on the dig that he was very practical, and not afraid of hard work or getting his hands dirty. I also saw him move some rubble while no one else was watching and he demonstrated a rugby player's strength which surprised me. Now, sitting opposite me, his loose wool jumper camouflaged any physicality.

"I can point you towards some Lincolnshire history, but there were Catholics, Protestants, Plantagenet and Tudor supporters and later Puritans all mixed together, feuding, seizing each other's land, killing each other or changing allegiances as the wind shifted."

"I think Sir Nigel suspects that the owners of Bickering Hall were Catholics into the mid-sixteenth century," I ventured.

"I'm sure he'd like to think that," Max said, dismissively. "He's a left-footer, so that element of treachery would appeal to him."

He paused and reflected a moment.

"Of course, he may be right," he conceded. "Did April know nothing about the hall's history?"

I shook my head.

"I'll email you the names of a few good books on the area," Max said. "All sorts of people were messing around, including the Suffolks. Their lands were all over the place."

"Not the Duke of Norfolk's?" I asked, remembering the only noble recusants to more or less survive.

Max laughed.

"Not that I know of."

256

Our meals arrived and we ate quietly, commenting only on the food. It was a congenial, good-humoured silence, and I think we enjoyed our meals very much.

When we'd finished, Max checked his watch, but made no move.

"You have to get back to work?" I asked.

"I should go soon, but no rush. I'm working on an application for funding for a dig in Cumberland."

"Cumberland? What's up there?"

"No idea. That's why I want to dig."

Max didn't often joke, so not only was the remark amusing but also unexpected.

"Do you want dessert or coffee?" he asked. "I have time for that."

"Not for me," I said, and thought he looked disappointed. It was only for an instant, so I wasn't sure.

I asked for the bill and after a brief exchange, paid it.

"I asked you," I said, hoping I didn't sound too much like a teacher.

"The maps and papers are in the car."

His old Land Rover didn't look like it had been cleared out since he left Cambridge. Books, maps, and various bits of equipment were piled in the back: shovels, sieves, a metal detector, buckets and trowels.

The papers for me were on the front seat, so he didn't have to dig for them.

"Apart from the two books, everything is a photocopy, so you can send them to Sir Nigel or throw them away," he said. "I hope he finds them useful for whatever he's looking for."

∞

When I got home, I put the maps and books on the table and walked to the window to look at the garden. It wasn't big, but it had given me something to do over the past few years. It was sunny, so I decided to make a start pruning the roses.

I know much has been written about when to prune roses, but the fact is that it doesn't actually make much difference as long as it gets done. I like to give them a prune in November and another in late March or early April. They flower well and don't get leggy. I also read that cutting them carefully on an angle just above a node isn't thought to matter much anymore and that an electric hedge-trimmer does just as well, but I think they deserve a bit more care, so, taking my secateurs, I set to work.

Though my mind was not filled with much, I found the physical work outside refreshing and continued until the light faded. I put the cuttings into a pile where I'd let them dry before burning them in the cottage's wood stove in a few days. I didn't often have a fire but had plenty of wood and sometimes one needed cosiness.

Returning inside, I realised how chilly it had become outside and went upstairs to have a shower. It was warming and refreshing, and I was feeling better about the world when I stepped back into my bedroom and was confronted by The Dress hanging before me.

I dried my hair and began to dress when I decided to grasp the moment and see if it still fit. To my amazement, it did, and I swayed and turned in front of the mirror admiring the way it hung and moved. The satin caught the light from the small lamp on the dressing table and seemed to magnify it into a warm glow.

I was reflecting that it was curious that the dress had no memories for me apart from being bought and wondered what future, if any it might have, when I was startled from my reverie by three sharp knocks on my front door.

I rushed downstairs and opened the door.

"Detective Inspector Covell!" I said, in surprise.

"Mrs Rawding."

Chapter Twenty-seven

Saturday
Rachel's Notebook

The look on the inspector's face when I opened the door can only be imagined, and I blush when I think of it. Wet hair, fluffy pink slippers and an elegant yellow ball dress. Did this constitute suspicious behaviour?

"Please come in, Inspector," I said stepping back and opening the door further. "I'm sorry for the way I look. I can explain – "

"I'm sure you can," he said, with a laugh, "but it's not at all necessary – and please call me Peter. This isn't an official visit."

We went into the sitting room.

"I'll be a minute. Let me change," I said, and beat a hasty retreat. When I returned, I tried to act more competent.

"If this isn't an official visit, can I offer you a drink? A beer? Gin and tonic?"

"A gin and tonic would be nice," he said.

Most of the things were in a corner cupboard in the sitting room, so I only had to leave for the tonic and ice.

I explained about the shower and the dress and told him about the portrait. I was half expecting a remark to the effect that if I could look as good as the dress, I might be worth painting, but he took a different tack.

"Was it Marissa's portrait that inspired this decision?" he asked.

"It's good, isn't it?" I said. "Actually, it was Ligeia Gordon's. I only saw it in the papers and magazines, but it made a big impression. When I met Ligeia – Sophie – and Sir Nigel, I thought it might be an interesting experience, and it would be nice if a few people knew what I looked like in my prime."

He laughed, having taken my explanation as I intended.

"You know," he began, more seriously, "Paul is still missed and talked about. He was good at his job and well-liked."

He paused, sensitive to my feelings.

I gave him a smile.

"That's about the best way to be remembered."

"I'm sorry – "

"Don't be," I said, gently. "Now, what brings you to Bardney, if nothing official."

He looked at his drink.

"Well, semi-official," he said. "I wanted to confirm that the pistol you found was nothing to do with the skeleton. And, as you probably know, the skeleton is nearly a hundred years older than the pistol. We will be returning the bits and pieces of iron and brass that were gathered to Marissa – but not the skeleton."

"And where will that go"?

Covell chuckled.

"Ah, well, you know police work. There's a form. . . and a process. . . and all the historical societies will get involved and the bones will sit in a box in an evidence locker for a few years and then be quietly buried with other unknown remains.

"That's sad," I said. "They don't even get a 'John Doe' identification. You don't have any idea who he was or how he died?"

He shook his head.

"There wasn't even agreement as to the sex."

"It could have been a woman?" I asked, surprised.

"People were smaller. Diets were different. For a scattered skeleton, it's hard to tell. One ilium was broken with a piece missing, and the other could have been a large woman or an average man."

I thought about this.

"Why is the idea of it being a woman so much more intriguing?" I asked.

"Oh, do you find it so?" Covell asked with a straight face. "Why is that?"

I was taken aback by the question, then I saw he was teasing. I smiled at him, and he returned it.

"You're right, though," I said. "It *is* more intriguing."

He said nothing for a while but enjoyed his gin and tonic.

"Do you know if Marissa intends to continue the work at the site?" he asked.

"I don't think she knows," I said. "It's all clear now anyway, isn't it?"

I told him I'd spoken to April and had had lunch with Max but neither seemed to know Marissa's plans.

"With the excavation done, it becomes a research project to determine what the building was," I said. "Growing up, we always called it the old barn. I only saw it driving by with my parents and it never occurred to me that it was anything else. It was so overgrown, we couldn't see much."

"That's the way I remember it, too," Covell said. "Without that to occupy her, what do you suppose Marissa will do?"

A faint glimmer sparked in the back of my mind. Was the reliable Detective Inspector here doing groundwork on Marissa? Was this part of an early stage of an inquiry that was part of some crime or was his interest more personal? A pretty heiress with an ancestral home would attract attention.

"Again, I can't tell you much," I said. "She was always ambitious, but once she'd achieved something, she'd move on. She qualified as an FRICS only a year before she left the estate agency.

"She never said so, but I suspect she had the idea of publishing a book about the dig with the additional kudos of having Sir Nigel's pictures.

"Now that she has the finds back, and Sir Nigel is doing the pictures, she may pursue that."

Covell had come to the end of his gin and, it seemed, his conversation. We sat in companionable silence until it grew embarrassing.

"Thank you, Mrs Rawding," he said, standing. "I'll let you get back to your evening – and your yellow dress – which looked wonderful."

෨

I hadn't expected his levity and compliment, and I had a good laugh as he left. On reflection, it was the sort of old-fashioned friendly visit that people used to make. Drop in unexpectedly, have a cup of tea or a drink, a brief chat and then go. It was rather what I had done with April, though I had arranged that in advance.

So, was he trying to find out about Marissa, or was there something he expected me to reveal? He hadn't tested my availability, and I wasn't sure how to take that.

Not that I knew what it was.

After supper, I debated emailing Sir Nigel, but in the end, thought he might enjoy personal contact and called him up.

He sounded much happier than when I'd last spoken to him.

"I am in less pain," he said. "The hospital removed the cast – which was for immobilisation more than bone-setting and have given me a tight boot which looks ridiculous, but does mean I can move around more easily. As a result, I only have two more watercolours to complete. One is pencilled and the other is inked, so the end is in sight.

"Now, what have you been up to?"

I had kept to my resolution about brevity and made bullet points. I had just begun telling him about my lunch with Max when Sir Nigel interrupted.

"I'm still waiting for your photographs," he said, gently reminding me.

"I'm so sorry! I took them over a week ago and never sent them. You'll have them tonight!

"I will also post you some maps that Max gave me. He said they're copies, so you can write on them," I said. "He also gave me two books on Lincolnshire history, but I'll bring them down when I come.

"I tried on the dress today, and it should do very well for the portrait."

I then moved on to tell him about the other things I'd learned so far, and what I planned to do the following week. He made listening noises and I suspected he was making notes as I spoke.

So much for the bullet points. It just all flowed out. Eventually, I came to the end, finishing with an apology that I hadn't accomplished more.

"You have done what I asked, Mrs Rawding," he said. "Thank you.

"Are you free the week after next? If so, we can get the portrait underway. I can build the background and sketch in your pose once I have the photographs," he said.

"Yes, I can do that. I'll call my friend and see if her spare room is still available."

We said goodnight. I mixed another gin and tonic and settled back on the old soft chintz sofa. What was I doing having conversations with a famous painter? What would my friends in the English department say? Trips to London, portraits and intrigue.

I knew what they'd say: nothing.

They just wouldn't believe me.

Chapter Twenty-eight

Thursday

A large envelope full of maps, charts and photographs arrived on Wednesday from Rachel. I called her up to acknowledge its arrival and left a message. She's done very well, both with the photographs and the research.

Speaking to her, I had the feeling that she still felt she hadn't accomplished much, but she has done much more than I expected she'd be able to.

The photographs she sent made me itch to get back to my studio, and today, with the aid of a taxi, I managed to get there. I began blocking the portrait. She had sent photographs of the whole room – I was very glad she printed them and hadn't just emailed them – and suggested that I could move furniture and other objects to suit the painting.

Looking at them, I fancied I could have chosen this room as belonging to her, as in some television competition that invades people's privacy. There was an unfussy neatness about it, a quiet self-assurance, and everything I could see looked like it had been deliberately chosen and placed.

With the aid of the sketches I had made when she was in London, I was able to block her into the room, though I had to guess the height of the room. After fiddling a bit, I decided to take a slightly downward look at her rather than the more usual head-on view. This removed any hint of a ceiling and consequently, made the room appear to be taller without actually painting it that way. I could always change it if she hated it.

Working on Rachel's portrait was a self-indulgent treat as I had not yet finished the watercolours. There were still two left to complete. One was nearly done, but the final one I'd spoiled and decided to start again. It had been a long time since I'd spoiled a painting, but given the time it had been since I was using watercolours, I expected to spoil a few. This one I damaged at my set, working at the dining table. I had my foot up on one of the other chairs and a sudden twinge of pain – twinge is the wrong word; hot iron spike would be more accurate – caused my hand to jerk and drop a large drop of dark green splash onto one of the figures. I tried the usual blotting tricks and diluting the area, but it made a worse mess and the surface of the paper began to become fibrous. There's no way back from that.

Not being mobile, I worked through lunchtime and called a taxi to take me home. I was exhausted by the time I entered my set but felt satisfied with the day's work: Rachel's portrait was blocked in, another watercolour was finished, and I'd made a start on the remake of the final one.

To mark that achievement, I put my feet up (carefully) and, almost instantly, fell asleep.

ය

I woke to hear Sophie in my kitchen opening a bottle of wine. At least I hoped it was Sophie. Albany doesn't get many intruders and only a small number of them open bottles of wine before stealing them or coshing the residents.

I heard her put the bottle and glasses on the dining table, then some paper rustling. I assumed she was looking at the maps and documents Rachel had sent.

"Anything interesting?" I asked, joining her after I'd put myself back together.

"Yes. The Merlot has an especially cheeky precocity," she said, barely looking up from a map.

I sat at the place where she had placed my glass and put my leg up on an extra chair. It wasn't hurting, but it made me remember to be careful when moving it.

"Cheers," I said, trying the wine.

The familiar taste told me that Sophie had opened one of mine.

"Good choice."

Her look told me that she knew exactly what I meant.

"Your new little girlfriend has been busy," she said.

"She sent me pictures of her home, too," I replied. "I left them at the studio."

"I bet she's still locked in Laura Ashley mode," Sophie said.

Her cattiness was only to try to provoke me into being pompous, pious or defensive of someone who was not there; it had absolutely nothing to do with the target.

I liked Rachel's frankness; it was a welcome relief from the vacillating affectations and pseudo-infatuation of Marissa. Although it was difficult, I managed not to rise to the bait.

"You'll have to wait to see the portrait," I said, debonairly drinking some wine. "Problems at the rehearsal? Your levels of vitriol only rise for a reason and neither Mrs Rawding – nor I – have provided you with one."

"You're getting close now," she retorted, mimicking my ironic tone. "But if you don't stop your Noel Coward impersonation, you'll have to cook your own supper!"

Sophie was in and out of the kitchen as she spoke. She was cooking one of her standards, and, in time a simple steak with mushrooms and pan-fried potatoes and some frozen peas appeared.

She sat down but had a quizzical look on her face, as though she were trying to remember if she'd forgotten something. After a moment she relaxed with a loud sigh.

"It was the admiral's turn to blow up today. Charles Grayson is a brilliant character actor who is never out of work because he can be hilarious or tear-jerkingly tragic as the role demands. He's not a method actor but studies his characters carefully and thoroughly. In this case, when Tony told him to do something that a senior Royal Navy officer would never do, he vociferously rebelled."

I had seen Grayson in a number of plays and in many television dramas, and while I confess that I'd never given him much thought, realised that what Sophie said was true: his characters had a very real feeling to them.

Grayson was about my age, and Sophie had told me that when a young actress, he had been kind to her and quietly protective. They shared a view of acting as a profession that required hard work to do well, and neither expected special privileges for doing it. He was happily married, and he would bring his wife – and sometimes his children, when they were old enough – to rehearsals, productions or film sets. As an actor, he knew what he was good at and stuck to it, seldom leaving his comfort zone, though when he did, I thought he did very well.

"What did the director want him to do?" I asked, wondering what scope there was to do anything offensive in *Relative Values*.

"Tony wanted the admiral to slap one of the characters on the back at their first meeting. Charles argued that the admiral would never dream of doing that. Tony exploded and asked him who was directing the play. 'God knows!' Charles countered and went home."

I was used to theatrical dramas, wounded egos and petulant behaviours, and was very glad that Sophie almost never protested direction. When she did, it was in private, and since she was now in the topflight, she usually got her way.

She *is* topflight: she'd won just about every acting award and her position was sealed with her DBE in one of the Queen's last honours lists. However, she would not have put herself in that category. She still genuinely believed that when she was asked to read for a part that there was a real chance of her not getting it.

Sophie would decline to read, or turn down roles if she genuinely felt she couldn't do them well, or simply didn't like the role. She did not need to be the star, and having outgrown the *ingenue* roles, she felt that her younger colleagues were the real stars. Also, as I have previously noted, if she liked a part and the play, she'd happily take the role of someone who was killed or disappeared after the first act.

"So, what's going to happen to Charles?" I asked.

"Well, when Tony left, he said he'd be calling the producers, though my feeling is that they will back Charles and we'll be getting a new director."

This was something that didn't happen often and plays that underwent such changes halfway through rehearsals seldom did well. Often, someone with little experience would be brought in to keep costs down, or someone dragged out of retirement.

"Do you think the production is in danger?"

"I don't think so," she replied, calmly. "It's an experienced cast and company. I've worked with many of them before. We're not under great pressure. We try it out in Guilford and Manchester with ten performances in each, then move to London for the tourist season. Even with Tony directing, we probably could have made it work, so all's not lost whether he returns or not."

I poured the last of the wine while Sophie cleared the table and put on the coffee. Since my fall, we sat at the table at ninety degrees to each other, not at opposite ends. It kept the wine bottles within reach of both of us.

"There was one production," Sophie continued, "where at the end of the run, Peter Barkworth presented the director with a bottle of vintage champagne. It was the final performance of *Crown Matrimonial.* He said, 'Well, we could have done it without you, but it wouldn't have been as much trouble.'"

I laughed, struggling not to choke on the wine.

"You weren't in *Crown Matrimonial*!" I exclaimed, still laughing. "You were barely nine years old."

"I didn't say I was there," she snapped. "Amanda Reiss told me when we did *The Rivals* together, years later. She had played the Queen Mother-to-be. She told me that when Barkworth said it, Wendy Hiller couldn't stop laughing."

"That's the sort of line I'd like to use on varnishing days with some of my subjects," I said.

She nodded.

"I've wanted to say it often."

Over coffee, I asked if she'd seen anything interesting on the maps Rachel had sent.

"The one I was looking at was from about 1750 and it didn't look like much of a place. There were a few names on the fields, then 'ruins of' the priory and the hall. An inn, a windmill, a forge and a few other things marked just as 'ruins' makes it sound like a pretty desolate place," she said.

"It must have been pretty bleak in November," I said. "Mind you, in those days, most places were."

I must have made a face after I spoke because Sophie asked if I were in pain.

"No, I was just thinking that I should call Marissa and ask her if she wants me to frame her pictures."

Chapter Twenty-nine

Friday
Rachel's Notebook

𝕴 was surprised to hear from Sir Nigel again after his call yesterday to say that he'd received my parcel. He asked if it would be possible to check at a library in Lincoln about changes to road layouts. Neither of us thought the highways department's records would go that far back and that the local history section of the library might yield a result.

He didn't explain why he wanted this, but he did offer to pay travel expenses and lunch. It will be a good excuse to visit the school and see some old friends. It will also give me the chance to think about their suggestion to return to teaching.

This portrait thing is throwing up all sorts of logistical problems. While I can stay with Jenna again, getting my dress and shoes to London on the train and then to Sir Nigel's studio could be a problem. I wonder if he has an iron. And what about my hair?

While I tell myself this is silly as he's painted hundreds of people in all sorts of uniforms and ceremonial dress, me and a yellow frock won't be something he'd worry about.

I'm finding this weird as I'm not usually vain. I expect having had some male conversation this week has something to do with it. I'll get more of that Monday when I visit the school.

CR

Tuesday

Rachel's Notebook

Visiting old friends at the school yesterday made me realise how much I missed being there. The friendships, the debates, the banter and watching the children learn and grow in spite of their obsessions with the latest trends, feuds, squabbles and other problems.

Shortly before I left, Marjorie, the head of English, and I had a serious talk. I'd always got on well with her and we shared a lot of laughs as well as hard work. She didn't suffer fools gladly, but could be very forgiving, too.

After filling her in on what I'd been up to in recent weeks ("Whatever prompted you to get yourself painted? Planning on presenting it to the school library?") She also had some choice comments about me mucking about in a dig, but the story of the old pistol evened the score.

Then she offered me a job for September. The second in the department – who had come since I left – was on the move again to take up a head of department's post somewhere ghastly. The job would be to replace him, as there would be no internal candidate since the most likely contender was due to retire at the end of the summer term.

This was the first direct and formal offer I had received, and, considering I hadn't taught in five years, was wholly unexpected.

I am going to have to give this serious thought. The post will have to be advertised, but if I apply, I've got a pretty good chance unless someone exceptional applies. While I gave the idea an enthusiastic reception when it was put to me, it's not a spur of the moment decision to make.

After visiting the school, I think I managed to track down the information Sir Nigel wanted and was able to photograph several old maps with my phone which I have already sent him.

I wanted to get to Jenna's house near Broomfield Park. It was straight down the A1, but I wanted to get there in daylight. I was dreading the trip on the underground with my dress bag, handbag and the books Max had given me. At least Jenna had said she'd give me a lift to the Underground station. There'd be more than a dozen stops and a quarter mile walk from London Bridge Station to Sir Nigel's studio when I would arrive looking just as I wanted to for posterity. Marjorie's astonishment came back to me: What *was* I thinking?

 છ

Things did come together, sort of.

I arrived – in the light – and managed to find a parking space not far from Jenna's house. I'd known her since we did our teacher training together nearly two decades ago. We were sent to the same grim school for teaching practice. The other teachers dumped their worst classes on us and disappeared. It's not the way it's supposed to work, but it's the way it does. We learned to swim very quickly, and after two weeks of sleepless hell, actually began to enjoy it. The students concluded that we weren't going to be scared away easily and gave up and carried on with their normal level of mayhem.

Jenna and I did a demonstration of stage fighting to break up the teaching of *Macbeth*, and – although we nearly killed each other – the children were convinced it was all just realistic acting.

Jenna shared the house with a friend, Marie, who was also a teacher. Whether this was a convenient way of living or something more, I didn't ask, and Jenna didn't tell; in the few nights I'd spent there, I hadn't succeeded in determining whether they had individual rooms.

That night I only saw Jenna. There was a parents' evening at school. Marie had stayed at the school and Jenna had only come home to let me in.

"Sorry, Rach! I've got to get back. The number of a good Chinese takeaway is on the dining room table," she said, hurriedly. "Order whatever you want. They'll deliver, and I'll buy you dinner. With luck we'll be back by ten. Don't worry if you're too tired to wait up."

I didn't see much more of her, though we did have a whisky when she got home and she ate the remains of my Chinese. Her face and body language contained all the exhaustion and frustration that I remembered from parents' evenings. I knew Jenna would want to unburden herself of the endless requests, complaints and excuses she'd heard all evening, and it was easy enough for me to listen.

In the morning, I bundled my dress, shoes, large handbag and the books into Jenna's Smart car and hoped the dress would be wearable when I got to Southwark.

"The station isn't far, so walking home shouldn't be a problem," she said. "It's safe enough around here. You're not going to be late, are you?"

"If I am I'll take a taxi from the station."

"And you've got your key?"

"Yes, Mum, and my homework and lunchbox."

ॐ

People with any sort of luggage are not appreciated on the Underground during the morning rush hour. I wanted to stand so I could hold the dress bag up, but with doors in the middle and at both ends of the car, it wasn't easy to keep out of the way.

I navigated the change and found myself at London Bridge station shortly after nine: too early to go to the studio.

I started out for Sir Nigel's, looking for a place I could sit down and get a cup of decent coffee and something to eat. The station offered only mobile food, and my first hundred yards down Tooley Street seemed to have only fried chicken, burgers and souvlaki. Then, tucked in a side street was a doorway that looked like something from Diagon Alley with a door in a cut-off corner, and dark green wooden exterior panelling.

A neatly painted gold lettered sign proclaimed "Southwark Tea & Coffee Company." A glance in the window showed diners with full English breakfasts and a selection of pastries. There were even coat hooks where I could hang the damn dress.

Half an hour later, I felt restored enough to move on.

Sir Nigel welcomed me with more coffee, croissant and *pain au chocolat*. Before preparing to be painted, we sat and chatted. I gave him the books and the pages of notes I had made at the library. He still didn't tell me what he was looking for, but I felt he would when he was ready.

"Are you able to get around better?" I asked, looking at the curious boot he was wearing.

He pointed to the cane standing by the doorway.

"For short distances," he said.

He showed me the finished watercolours which I thought captured the experience. I could recognise the various people working with Max and Marissa directing and supervising. It was clever the way Sir Nigel had been able to convey serious work being done and also the happy atmosphere that I remembered as the main element of the dig.

He also showed me the quick sketches of all of us. In these, the faces were more important than the work being done whereas it was the opposite in the main series.

I looked at the one of me and was surprised.

"Is that what I look like to you?" I asked.

"Not just to me," he said. "Take it into the bathroom and look at it in the mirror."

Seeing my face looking back at me from the small square of paper in the mirror, I wondered how I'd cope living with a metre square painting.

In a few moments, I'd be fixing my hair, doing my makeup and putting on the dress and shoes, but in the drawing, I had no makeup on and thought I looked better.

I went back into the main room and sat down.

"If it's all right with you, we can work on the painting this morning until around noon, then order some lunch. There's an Italian restaurant that delivers just down the road.

"While we're waiting for it, we can go over what you've found," he said. "Then, if you want to go out for a bit – fresh air or some shopping – you can do that, but we should start again by two.

"You can let me know when you want to take a break. I'm apt to just go on painting, but standing still can be tiring."

His manner was light-hearted but I thought he seemed tired. Not getting his usual walk to work seems to have slowed him down.

"You'd better get changed into your glad-rags," he said. "I should have borrowed an iron from Sophie. If you need one, I can have her bring it around at lunchtime."

"Isn't she rehearsing?" I asked.

"Ah. That tale will take too long to tell," he replied. "Maybe over lunch."

Chapter Thirty

Wednesday
Rachel's Notebook

Sir Nigel waited patiently for me to prepare myself and dress. When I looked at myself in the full-length mirror (with additional lights that illuminated me from top to toe), once again, I wondered what I was doing.

When I emerged, Sir Nigel smiled and said:

"Now, that was worth waiting for!"

With that, I regained my confidence, and walked to the corner of the room near where we'd been sitting and Sir Nigel directed my pose. What looked to me like improvisation, I later realised had been carefully constructed to fit in with preparation he had done using my photographs.

He had cleared the top of a low book case and put a plank across it, supported by a number of books.

"I want to get the height so that it's as close to the dresser at your house as possible while making your reach graceful."

"If you are happy with the idea, I want to capture you in the middle of picking something up," he explained. "You'd be turning back and looking up to the person entering the room, or speaking to you."

I nodded, not quite understanding what I might be picking up.

"Think of picking up a gold necklace, or a pearl choker," he said. "You're nearly ready to go to the ball, but you want one more ornament."

This I understood.

"There is a danger here and that's that you look like you've been caught purloining something," he said, and we both laughed. "But, of course, what you are really picking up is the viewer."

Crafty old man.

"We want you placed so that your neck, hair and both eyes are visible and that the dress can be appreciated, too," he added.

I gathered he meant that something of my figure could be seen. Yet, there was no innuendo about Sir Nigel, he just knew what made a good painting.

As he told me how to stand, extend my arm, turn and lift my head, he could have easily touched me to move me into position, but he did not. Each subtle placement of my arms and legs, each twist and turn of my torso had been rehearsed in his head, and he was bringing my image to life.

He took a few pictures, but didn't look at them. He also took pictures of my feet. This I found was to help me recreate the pose after resting or on subsequent days. The rug I stood on had a geometrical pattern. I later learned it was a hundred and fifty-year-old Persian rug.

Nearly half an hour later, he said I could relax. He caught my glance at the sofa, then passed me the high stool that was near his easel.

"Thanks, I don't want to mess up the dress any more than necessary," I said. I immediately hoped I didn't sound like a dumb clothes-horse.

Before sitting down, I retrieved a bottle of water from the small fridge, as Sir Nigel scrolled through the photos. After a few minutes, he handed me the phone. I scrolled through them and found he had deleted about ninety percent of them, and only six remained.

I spent some time looking at them, not from vanity, but in fascination of his thought process. I gave him his phone back.

"The hand isn't right," he said, and went to his chest of drawers and began looking for something. He found a small box and rooted about some more until he found a small brass chain, slightly longer than a choker. He put the box on the plank and gave me the chain.

"Don't worry, I will paint it as gold, not brass," he said. "Now, look."

He showed me the picture of my hand reaching down to pick something up.

"Now, hold the chain in your fingers, but turn your hand up."

He regarded my wrist and hand.

"Let a little more of the chain fall."

I did.

"You see? Now you are selecting something, not acting like a cat burglar."

I looked at my hand. The gesture was so similar but so different. I looked at Sir Nigel and smiled.

"Holding it that way is much more active," he said. "The intention of the other movement is vague. You are a lady who knows what she wants, but you seldom tell anyone."

That made me catch my breath. I'm not used to near-strangers being so perceptive. This being painted lark is suddenly more interesting and worth the time with the road maps.

We put the pose back together. He gave me the picture of my feet so I could place them, and once I did, the rest of the pose came surprisingly easily. The slightly raised hand also felt better, and I told him.

"If you have a piece of jewellery that you'd like me to include, bring it to Varnishing Day and I'll paint it in."

At about quarter to twelve, Sir Nigel called the Italian restaurant and ordered our lunches. While he did that, I had time to change back into my street clothes and sit on his sofa and rub my feet.

"I tell subjects that I expect them to work as hard as I do," he said, handing me a cold drink. "They don't know what I mean until the first session is over."

Because he had set up the corner for my pose, he had moved his armchair from its usual place to the other end of the sofa. He put his leg up on the sofa and leaned back, stretching.

"This isn't at all as I imagined it," I said. "It's funny how you can have such strong pre-conceived ideas about things you know nothing about. It's the sort of prejudice that I used to get teaching: 'I hate Jane Austen.' Oh, yes? How many have you read?"

This amused him, but rather than picking up Jane Austen, he asked me what my favourite play was. While I adjusted to the question and tried thinking of an answer, Sir Nigel said:

"Let me guess: *The Tragical History of Doctor Faustus*."

My mouth opened but nothing came out.

"How did you guess that?" I asked, once I recovered my voice.

"It's concise, no nonsense, imaginative, epic in impli-cation and the language is clean but powerful," he said.

Then I burst out laughing.

"You've met one of my students or colleagues!"

"If I did, I doubt we'd talk about Christopher Marlowe," he said. "No, I heard you joking about the walls of the ruin."

I laughed.

"I remember. I said they were hardly the topless towers of Ilium."

I was about to ask how he became familiar with the play when the food arrived. He handed me a fiver and I went to the door to collect our meals.

Eating was a bit precarious as the table was small and there were several boxes of food and our plates were large. The table was by the window at the far end of the room, so I was able to see the painting for the first time.

I actually wondered who the elegant lady was. The suggestion of my sitting room gave me the familiar context, but it was hard to believe that I was looking at myself.

When he came to the table with napkins and cutlery, he caught me staring at my image.

He transferred the food onto the plates.

"I wish I knew how you can cook pasta so that even after it's been delivered, it's just like it came straight from the kitchen," he said.

The food was very good. We didn't say much but the silence was comfortable. When we finished, he caught me looking at the painting again. It had been distracting me throughout the meal.

He took the plates to the sink, seeming to move with little discomfort.

"Something's bothering you," he said.

It wasn't a question or a challenge.

"You're not happy with something? Don't worry, it's not unusual," he said, gently. "I can change most things; we can start again, or you can simply stop the process and go back to Lincolnshire."

I could feel my face flush – and it was hard to remember the last time *that* happened. He was right: I was unhappy with something. The trouble was, I didn't know what, but something in the painting – even in it's unfinished state – wasn't quite right.

"Does that really happen?" I asked. "Someone pulling the plug on a painting?

"I mean, I love this, but something's not working and I can't tell what," I said.

This sounded feeble even to me. I was terrified of trying to tell one of the best portrait painters in London to change something. He'd painted *everyone* and I was a former teacher from nowhere.

Sir Nigel's manner hadn't changed a bit: he was still calm and friendly, but I began to worry when he began unscrewing the top fitting to the easel.

"Let me show you something," he said, taking the picture down and putting it into one of the slots in his cupboard.

He withdrew another painting and fixed it in the easel. I recognised the person immediately. He saw my face light up.

"You recognise poor Fletcher Bailey," he said. "I was sorry to hear of her death. I did this several years ago when she did her London show.

"The painting is unfinished because she broke *her* ankle and went back to the United States."

"I didn't realise you painted American celebrities," I said. "It was a shame about her tour. What was she like?"

I remembered Fletcher Bailey's ill-fated tour. Special effects didn't work, and she fell and broke her leg or something and most of it was cancelled.

"Did you ever hear her sing? Go to a performance?" I asked.

Sir Nigel shook his head.

"Although this painting was never finished, while it was being done, she secretly commissioned a smaller painting from me. She loved that little one," he indicated a small picture of a figure sleeping on the grass. "She wanted one of the same size and style. For herself. It was as if it would be a secret from her manager and handlers.

"She contrived to come for a few sittings and I delivered the painting to her very shortly before she fell and went home."

He laughed.

"She came – looking like that – then went into the bedroom and came out twenty minutes later looking like a very small, mousy little girl – and that's how I painted her.

"The sessions were quite short because it took her so long to get her makeup off and remove her hair bits."

"What will you do with the painting?" I asked.

"She didn't pay for it, so it's mine, but it's been in that cupboard for six years. I got it out to look at again when I heard of her death. Funny. No one else knows it exists."

For some reason, I was moved by the thought of the young death and the unfinished portrait.

"A portrait from life," I mused. "You did finish it, though."

"I don't like not finishing things."

He took the picture of Fletcher Bailey down and put it away and replaced it with me. I went into the bedroom, fixed my makeup and got back into the shoes and dress.

"So, we're continuing?" Sir Nigel asked when I came out.

"Thank you for showing me that picture," I said. "You made me realise what I wasn't happy with. It's the hair."

Sir Nigel smiled as if he knew all along that it was the hair that was the problem.

"You've made me look elegant, but something – well, the rhythm was wrong."

"Rhythm?" he asked.

"Sorry. English teacher again. When a poet wants you to look at a line or phrase, he breaks the rhythm to draw attention to it," I said, and he nodded. "On the other hand, sometimes it's inept poetry."

"Or inept painters?"

He was joking. I hope.

"Maybe sometimes, but in this case it's an inept sitter," I said. "Everything is elegant except my hair. If I'm about to put on jewellery, that means everything else is perfect – but it's not."

He was now in his armchair with his leg up on the sofa.

"And you will make it right, how?" he asked.

"I thought a French twist. Can you do that with what you've painted so far? I don't want you to start again."

He nodded, still smiling.

"Get yourself ready."

Chapter Thirty-one

Wednesday

Fixing Rachel's hair would be possible, but I'd have to do some careful scraping and overpainting which would take time. I decided to draw her head in pencil on paper and then do an oil sketch in burnt umber. She was much happier with the new look. I told her she could leave at around three and I could tinker with the portrait using the sketches.

I also told her – if she was pleased with the rest of the painting – that she could have tomorrow morning off and come at around one-thirty. I thought I could have all but the final details done by the end of that session.

"I'm looking forward to Varnishing Day champagne," she said, when she left.

It took half an hour or so to clean my brushes, put lids back on the various bottles and wash the dishes from lunch.

My ankle was hurting; it had been pretty good but I'd forgotten to take the paracetamol that appeared to be a consistent part of my current diet.

I went to the table and began looking at the maps and the books that Rachel had brought. I hadn't expected to find much about Bickering, but there was a section in one of the books about "The Lincoln Rising" that caught my eye.

In October 1536, more than twenty thousand people (possibly up to forty thousand) marched from towns around Lincoln to protest the dissolution of the monasteries along with the seizing of silver, gold crosses, jewels and church bells. Many of those protesting had contributed their groats for generations.

While doubtless there were rabble rousers and Plantagenet loyalists in the crowds, the protest was against the suppression of the monasteries, not against the king.

The Tudors were fiercely defensive of their position, and the wealth confiscated from the monasteries was already bankrolling their ambitions and finding its way into the pockets of their supporters, so retribution was swift and brutal.

Leaders were executed, lands and houses taken, and posts of responsibility stripped from the participants.

This looked like a clue worth following. If any names could be linked to the rising and Bickering Hall, I thought we'd have a plausible scenario for the proper historians to look into. I have no pretensions of being an historian, but I enjoy a puzzle.

There were a few other bits to resolve before I could close the Lincolnshire business.

෨

Thursday

It took nearly all my will power and a handful of paracetamol to get to the studio this morning.

In the evening, Sophie came at about seven and helped herself to a drink. I had just finished a small meal of an omelette and a few sausages. I was not ready to talk about my recent thoughts about Bickering, and she would not have appreciated a monologue about Rachel's hair. As a result, she did most of the talking.

The producers of *Relative Values* appeared to be starting to panic about not being able to find a replacement director. The cast was still being paid, there were rehearsal hall fees and a scheduled opening night.

"So relative values are declining sharply," I said.

"All might not be lost," Sophie said. "Gerald and Tom – the producers – asked to see me today. They're still paying me, so I went."

"Do you know them?"

"I've worked with them before," she said. "They don't often do West End productions; I get the feeling they do one every so often to let everyone know they're still around. They produced *The Philadelphia Story* that I did in Manchester, but TV and cinema advertisements are their bread and butter.

"Anyway, today, they asked if I would like to direct," she said, with a broad grin.

"Direct what?"

"Don't be obtuse! *Relative Values*. They really asked if I would take it over!"

I sat up.

"You could do it, you know."

"But not be in it; not the first time," Sophie said. "I did have an idea, though. Do you remember Jackie Streetly?"

I shook my head.

"She was in my year at RADA. She acted and made it really big for about fifteen years, then suddenly left the stage, taught drama somewhere and got married – which surprised me, but that's another story.

"Her husband died suddenly a year or two ago – I don't know the details, maybe he got Covid – anyway, I said she'd be worth talking to.

"Tom picked up the phone to his assistant, and after half an hour's searching and calling, got her on the line and handed me the phone. Of course, she remembered me.

"I gave the phone to Gerald who asked if she wanted to take over as director."

As she told her story, I began to recall who Jackie Streetly might be.

"Turns out she lives in Putney. Tom and Gerald wanted her to come to the office immediately. She told them she'd come in Monday morning."

I hadn't heard Sophie prattle like this in several years. It was an indication that she was happy, so I didn't mind listening.

Sophie and Jackie Streetly were more acquaintances than friends. At RADA, Jackie had noticed evidence of Sophie's abuse in her behaviour and obliquely indicated that she knew – first-hand – how she felt. Sophie had told me this years ago and never mentioned Jackie since except in a list of names. While active in the theatre, whenever Jackie met Sophie at an event, she'd always squeeze her hand in alliance, but they never shared their experiences. As a result, we were the only ones with an inkling of Sophie's history.

❧

Friday

On Friday morning, I called Helena Stirakis and told her that I was now able to receive Marissa's pictures. She proposed delivering them Monday, which would suit me well.

Getting to the studio Friday morning took some effort as the ankle was reminding me that it still wasn't up to normal use. It appears that old people's bones heal more slowly than in the young. Once at the studio, another dose of paracetamol reduced the *memento mori* for a few hours.

I had some time before Rachel arrived to finish the adjustments to her hair and fix the background and shadowing. Fortunately, her head was shown against a plain background which made it less fussy.

Rachel arrived promptly at nine-thirty. The earlier start was to enable her to head back to Lincoln and avoid the rush hour. She had managed to park not too far away.

She brought a few croissants and I made coffee while she changed.

"I'm getting used to wearing this dress, now," she said, from the bedroom.

"You will have to wear it out soon," I returned. "Once the painting has been shown, it will make you instantly recognisable."

She laughed.

"When word gets around, I'm dreading my old students going to the Summer Exhibition and torturing me about it in September."

"Have you decided to take the job, then?"

"I've been lonely and selfish for long enough now," she said, coming into the main room. "The dig showed me that I'm ready to re-join the world. I've decided and will visit the school when I get home."

I handed her the coffee and we walked to the canvas so she could inspect her new hairdo.

She smiled.

"I wish I looked that lovely," she said.

"Right now, you do and, when you get back in the world, a lot more people will know it, too."

She walked to her place and took the pose.

"What are you working on today?" she asked.

"The light on the folds and creases in the dress," I said. "So far, I have used seven different colour mixes of yellow, and think it will probably take another four to get it where I want it. Just keep your body still, but you can move your head and arms."

She was a good subject and stood in her pose for nearly twenty minutes. I gave her a break, but continued working while she moved around and then put her feet up on the sofa for a few minutes.

While she was doing that, I made some final adjustments to the highlights on her face and hair and warmed up the skin tones on her arms which had a more dramatic effect than I anticipated. This was the point where I had to be careful not to overdo it.

After relaxing for ten minutes, she stood again, and in the next twenty minutes, I completed the work on the dress.

It was all but done. It just needed her own piece of jewellery painted in.

I motioned for her to come forward to see it.

Reactions to pictures can be unsettling, yet I was always disconcerted when sitters confronted the finished portrait and seemed surprised when they had seen it every step of the way.

Rachel's eyes opened wide, but she said nothing. She said nothing for so long that I decided I should fill the gap.

"The reaching hand is empty," I began, stating the obvious. "When you come down for Varnishing Day in a week or two, you can bring a piece of your own jewellery – a necklace or bracelet, and I'll paint it in."

"When do you need to get this to the Royal Academy?" she asked.

"By the end of April."

"It is definitely going in?"

"Only if you want it to," I said, then added, "Don't you think it's good enough?"

Chapter Thirty-two

Monday

I pretty much hibernated from Thursday afternoon until Sunday. It takes a while to detach from a portrait, and this one had the additional accretions of historical intrigue. Though technically, I still had the jewellery to add, the picture was finished. Rachel's inability to express herself at seeing the finished product at first concerned me. She had changed into her street clothes before returning to look again.

"It would be nice if at least one person remembered me that way," she said.

That was enough to satisfy me. She left before lunch, and I made my way back to Albany. I dosed myself again, drank a quantity of water and lay down with my foot up on a pillow. I began reading about fifteenth and sixteenth century Lincolnshire until the paracetamol kicked in.

When I woke, I cooked a light supper before resuming reading and making notes. While there wasn't anything concrete, what I read gave some credibility to my suspicions and the "what" emerged. I would have to leave the "who" to those who knew better. I also harboured the unlikely fear that I could discover names of people who had been ancestors of people I knew and did not wish to stir up ancient animosities.

I texted Sophie not to come over. She immediately called to see if I was all right, and while not completely reassured, didn't come round until Sunday. By then, I had been through the relevant sections of the books, the maps and the information Rachel had got for me from the library.

Sophie had some charity do on Saturday and was out most of the day as well as in the evening. She dropped by after lunch on Sunday to help finish my bottle of wine but only stayed for an hour or so. The ankle was feeling better and I was determined not to let it get in the way of a trip I was planning but first, I had to receive Marissa's paintings back from the Courtauld.

Shortly before ten on Monday morning, my buzzer sounded and Helena's voice demanded admission. Guy Stone, the chief handler was with her and moved the paintings into the lift.

"We're parked on the pavement, so once these are in your studio and unwrapped, Mr Stone will head back," Helena said on emerging from the lift. "I'll stay because you and I have got to talk."

With the pictures moved into the studio and Guy on his way back to the Courtauld, I made Helena a coffee. She had a nose around while she waited. There were no paintings on my easel, so she was deprived of making any barbed work in progress comment. She did, however, stand in front of the small picture of Sophie sleeping on the grass at Versailles.

"I didn't know you did any small pictures," she said.

"I've just finished a set of half-imperial sheet watercolours," I said. "I use smaller sizes for personal work."

She continued to look at the picture.

"The face is cleverly disguised, but I'd be willing to bet that's Ligeia Gordon," she said.

"Not many people guess," I said.

Helena smiled.

I picked the Tudor portrait up and fitted it into the easel.

"The paintings of famous people have greater value than those of unknown ones," she said. "But, the unknown people are far more interesting.

"This poor girl – whoever she was – was in a family caught on the wrong side of history," she continued, wondering out loud. "How old do you think she is? Sixteen? Eighteen? Was she able to make a good marriage? That's more fascinating than all the deadly minor royals whose lives – even then – were documented to the last cutting remark."

Helena moved to where I had stood the flower painting on the floor and stared at it. I shuffled over and lifted it on the table.

"Can you put it on the easel?" she asked.

I removed the lady and tightened the flowers into place.

"These two pictures are remarkable and important," she began. "You still won't tell me where they came from?"

I shook my head.

"Nigel," she said, with all her professional presence, "you must convince the owners to make these public – or at least invite art historians and curators to see them.

"The flower painting and the lady are of *major* historical significance, if not artistic," she concluded. "The pub painting is amusing, but not important."

"That's where you are wrong, Dr Stirakis," I replied. "The pub painting is the key to the whole thing."

ॐ

The pub painting might not be the key to the whole thing, but I was sick of other people pronouncing on what was or was not important. I found that to be one of the advantages of portrait painting: conversations with people helped keep me out of the rarefied and self-important atmosphere that envelopes the art market and clouds judgement.

I knew Marissa was keen to receive the watercolours, and I still had a few of the individual working sketches to finish. Once they were done, I'd take them to her and arrange to meet Max at the site at the same time.

The final piece of that trip would be to meet Rachel. Before she left London, she asked if, rather than make a return trip with the piece of jewellery she'd be holding, she could give it to me while I was in the area. I could get Sophie to hold it to paint what I needed to finish the picture.

This was not entirely unusual. Several friends had donned uniforms, academic gowns, judicial robes and other clothing to enable me to finish a portrait without the main attraction. (It's remarkable how different a suit of armour looks when being worn compared to being mounted on a museum dummy.)

I worked until about two-thirty – foregoing lunch – on the pencil drawings before calling a taxi to take me back to Albany.

৪৩

I stayed holed-up in my set on Tuesday. The ankle was noticeably better which was very encouraging as I had a hospital appointment on Thursday. I was well-aware that a new level of pain would begin once I began physiotherapy and was told to do a lot of walking.

What I really wanted to be able to do was drive so I could lay the whole Bickering business to rest.

I telephoned Max and arranged to meet him at the site on the following Wednesday. Next, I called Marissa to let her know that I'd be returning her pictures and delivering the watercolours and the pencil sketches.

It took a while to get her off the phone. She wanted to tell me about her next project which was to do another dig around the periphery of Bickering Priory.

"A lot went on just beyond abbey walls," she said. "Workshops, farm buildings, residences, shops, and so on. We might find more there than on the first site."

She explained that she knew all the landowners and they had given permissions – with various restrictions and limits – to conduct geophysical surveys, metal detection and drone filming.

She told me in detail how she'd learned to operate a drone while working for the estate agency and now had her own vehicle.

When I called Rachel, she was delighted to hear I'd be coming and told me that she had a piece of her husband's grandmother's jewellery that she wanted in the portrait.

"I had been planning to wear it with the dress anyway," she said. "I think you'll find it a good piece to include."

She chatted for a while – though not nearly as long as Marissa had – and told me she had accepted the offer to return to Lincoln Minster School.

"I love the idea of being back there, but I've become very lazy," she said.

Even to me – who barely knew her – she sounded excited and much happier.

Thursday
Rachel's Notebook

All of a sudden, my life seems to be waking up. It started with the dig, meeting new people and talking to people I hadn't spoken to in years.

Then, there was the curious business of meeting Sir Nigel and Ligeia Gordon and later discovering that they knew Chief Inspector Warren.

The final thing (things) was the interest that Peter Covell suddenly seems to have in me. He asked me to dinner tomorrow, and I saw no harm in accepting. He's good company, and his work as a detective means that I understand his thought process. He has a strong protective instinct, which – having been on my own for so long – has a certain attraction, but I'm not sure I'd like that in the long run.

While my contact with Max was brief, at the dig, he seemed to take me seriously – even before I found the pistol parts – and he did later on when we met for lunch.

Paul had the ability to make me feel safe while letting me enjoy a sense of independence. I hated the secrecy of his work, and I don't know how interested he was in my school stories, but somehow, we could laugh at it and make it work.

But, I always feared for him.

The experience of being painted was yet another in the string of events that have led me to my present feelings. There's no doubt that there's a lot of vanity involved, but at the same time, it is a creative process. Something will be left behind to be considered in the future.

Hearing Sir Nigel speculate about the unknown woman in Marissa's painting made me think of what might happen to mine. How long will it survive? Why wasn't the name of the Tudor lady written on the back? Is there anyway of discovering who she was and what happened to her.

In his old-fashioned way, Sir Nigel assures me that the records of the Royal Academy will preserve my image and identity for centuries.

Now, I'm not actually sure that I like that idea.

I laugh at myself because, in a few months, my only worry will be what I'll teach Year 9 on Thursday.

Chapter Thirty-three

Wednesday

The quack said I'd be all right to drive but not to do too much walking. My various appointments were worked out and I agreed to meet Max Hillyard at the site at one. We'd then go to see Marissa, and then I'd stop at Rachel's before going to Horncastle for another night at the Captain John Smith.

Sophie had generously got up at the crack of dawn and accompanied me to the studio to help me load Marissa's paintings and drawings into the hire car when it came.

I find that as one gets older, the amount of stuff I think I need for a simple overnight multiplies alarmingly.

We had time for a brief coffee before the car arrived.

"You've been working very hard in spite of your foot," she said. "You ought to take yourself to Paris in a week or so and exercise the ankle in the Louvre."

"That's a very appealing idea," I said, "but I'm not sure I'm up to that yet."

"If you leave on a Friday, I'll come with you and come back on Sunday evening. Shall I make reservations?"

"Not yet, but soon."

◌₃

Traffic in London since the lockdowns had not fully recovered in volume. Emissions restrictions and the congestion charge further reduced the number of private vehicles. This meant that I was able to get onto the motorway in under an hour and into Horncastle by twelve-thirty.

The hotel was used to me by now and let me check in, leave my case in my room and freshen up before going to Bickering.

Once again, I had rented a small SUV to accommodate the pictures safely, and when I arrived at the site, I drove straight up the narrow track on the bramble-covered mound that overlooked the dig site and parked on top.

Max hadn't yet arrived, so I used the time to inspect the ruin and see it with the earth cleared down to the original floor. It was a patchwork of brick and stone, and, although uneven, was remarkably tight. Standing in it and looking at the few windows that had been unbricked, I felt that my guess about the building was essentially correct.

As I tried to imagine the shell as a complete building, I heard a car pull up and walked around to meet Max.

He came towards me as I approached and extended his hand. Marissa was at the rear of his car getting something from the boot. She stopped what she was doing and came to me, giving me a big hug and an unnecessary kiss.

"The stick is very *distingué*," Marissa said. "You should keep it."

She shivered against a sudden blast of wind.

"Is this going to take long, darling?" she asked. "Can't we do most of it over lunch back at the house?"

"Sir Nigel's driven from London to show us something," Max said, impatiently.

His manner was more teasing than rude, but I'd never heard him use anything but an affectionate tone with her before. She seemed unbothered, and continued her repartee. After a few minutes of chit-chat, I began walking up to my car. They followed, but I saw Marissa had brought her drone.

"The floor clearance looks great," I said. "Did they ever identify the skeleton?"

Max shook his head.

"That's still a mystery," he replied. "It's all still a mystery, and a lot of other things don't make sense yet, either.

"I may be able to help," I said, taking a deep breath. "I have no expertise, but I like puzzles and I have had time to think, and Rachel Rawding has been helping me with some research – things you didn't have time for, Max.

"What I think I have done is fix some points that people like you two will need to connect."

Both looked gratifyingly intrigued.

I went to the car and drew out the copy of the map that Rachel had found.

"What I need to ask you to do is visualise how things were four hundred years ago," I began. "As you both know, Bickering Priory was just there."

I pointed to an area across the street about a hundred yards along the lane.

"Also, as you know, there never seems to have been too much in Bickering," I continued. "It was more an area than a village. It encompassed the priory, an inn, farm buildings, a blacksmiths, and down the lane, near that clump of trees, a windmill."

"And Bickering Hall," Marissa added.

"And Bickering Hall," I repeated. "Now, here are the broad brushstrokes, or the dots to connect, if you prefer.

"This area supported the Yorkists and Plantagenets. Following the victory of Henry VII, things didn't change much as long as people didn't make trouble. The country was still Catholic and as long as taxes were paid and sedition was limited, private preferences enabled things to continue pretty much as they had.

"However, with the coming of Henry VIII and the dissolution of the monasteries, such tolerance did not continue.

"Now, by all accounts, Bickering Priory was no model of piety, and its administration shifted between religious orders several times. You could go to bed a Cistercian and wake up a Benedictine. Still, it was a small religious centre, and gave alms, provided pilgrims headed to Lincoln a place to stay and collected money."

"From what I can tell, the hall and lands were owned by the De Merveilleux family – "

"Ha!" Marissa exclaimed. "I was at school with a Clarissa de Merveilleux!"

"Well, they're still around," I said. "Was she Catholic?"

Marissa shrugged.

"We can ask her," Max said, to urge me to continue.

"Richard De Merveilleux took part in the Lincolnshire Rising in 1538 to protest the seizing of monastic lands and goods."

"Pretty brutally suppressed," Max said.

"Indeed. Richard was able to escape with his life, but his lands – including the hall – were forfeit," I said. "It appears to have passed into the Rawden family – which is probably a variation on Rachel's name – and the family kept it until it was burned sometime between 1580 and the Civil War."

This history lesson seemed to be boring Marissa and she fiddled with her drone controls, so I addressed Max.

"The Rawden's don't appear to have cared much about religion and either became non-conformists or were sympathetic to them because what we are looking at here is the ruin of an early non-conformist or Puritan chapel."

This got Marissa's attention back and she quickly looked up at me, and then at the chapel.

"I've found no evidence, but I think it was built – or at least enhanced – by bricks and stone from the hall."

Max nodded.

"We didn't find any heavy roof timbers because there weren't any," I continued. "I think this chapel – and the priory buildings and church – had thatched roofs that needed only slender poles."

"That would be consistent with what I was able to find out," Max said. "But how were you able to find out so much more than I did? I looked at the materials in detail before we started."

"Don't beat yourself up, Max," I said. "That's the difference between the amateur and the professional. You looked to see what was there, and you looked dispassionately, as you are supposed to. I, on the other hand, posited a theory and set out to prove it. I also had three key advantages that you didn't have."

"Which were?"

"Marissa's paintings."

"My paintings?" she asked.

"Will you humour me, Marissa?" I asked.

She nodded.

"Can you fly your drone down to where the windmill was and hover at about thirty feet."

"Get the tablet from the car, Max," she said, without taking her eyes off the drone as it headed down the lane.

"Do you film video or take pictures?" I asked her.

"I can do both."

Max returned with the tablet just as Marissa approached the site of the windmill.

"There?" she asked.

"A little further, I think."

We watched the small machine reach the small trees.

"There!" I said. "Now, can you take it to thirty feet?"

She deftly dropped the drone and pictures began to appear on the tablet.

"Point it more or less towards us," I instructed.

I watched the view I wanted begin to appear on the screen.

"Can you take a few pictures from that position?"

She pushed a button five times. Max did something on the tablet and showed me a still image.

"Yes. Good," I said. "Now, one more thing before we go to lunch: keep at about that height and angle the camera so you keep a bit of the ground in the picture. The horizon isn't important.

"Fly down the lane towards us and in a hundred feet or so, I'm going to ask you to turn off the lane and fly down this gap between us and the chapel."

While it looked like Marissa was concentrating hard, her control was easy and assured. Max and I kept our eyes on the tablet.

"Turn off the road now," I said, and within a few moments, the drone flew passed the chapel, then returned to where we were standing and dropped gently at Marissa's feet.

"Thank you, Marissa," I said. "Well done! I think we have just what we need."

She picked up the drone and switch off the control while Max shut down the tablet.

Marissa was about to start walking down the mound to her car then stopped and turned back to me.

"You've got the chapel, a windmill, the priory, an inn, but did you discover where Bickering Hall was? We've looked all over that field for years, haven't we, Max?" Do you know where it was?"

"What? Bickering Hall? Yes, of course," I said. "We're standing on it."

Chapter Thirty-four

Wednesday

*L*unch was the normal Bickering Place fare: soup, French bread, paté, cheeses, and some smoked ham. We sat around the kitchen table with April, while Marissa – surprisingly – served the soup.

I was now being besieged with questions, and Marissa had excitely told her mother that I had "discovered all sorts of things." Max and I were able to chat quietly while that briefing was going on, and I restated that much of what I had said was supposition.

"And that is why so many discoveries are made by amateurs," Max said, sadly. "They have a romantic vision, pieced together from evidence, while the professionals have to find much more evidence first."

"It's the same in many fields," I said. "The person who designs a concept car doesn't have to engineer it. I've just proposed a story suggested by the evidence. I don't pretend the research is anything but superficial, but after lunch, I'll show you all the paintings and you can decide whether this theory is worth following up."

April appeared to have no interest in the discussion about the ruin, hall, priory or inn. However, she did show some interest in the windmill. Marissa asked her if she'd known there was one, but April's reply was vague and she asked me a series of questions about Sophie, what she was working on, and whether she'd be coming to Lincolnshire anytime soon.

Marissa was tying to get her to listen to a list of names I'd given her to see if any rang a bell.

"Ackroyd, Ballen, Baxter, Crancy, De Marney, Fflyte, Gaspre, Hardison, Hepworth, Jaques, Krocker – "

April turned to her.

"I think the Gilliats bought the house from people called Jaques," she pronounced it as the character in *As You Like It*, Jake-wheeze. "I don't remember if they bought it or married into it."

"When was that?" Max asked.

"In the eighteenth century, not long after the house was rebuilt," April said.

"Do you have any papers?" Max asked, eagerly. "Sorry," he added, quickly. "This is exciting."

April laughed.

"I expect they're either in the estate office or with the solicitors," she said. "Marissa can look, if she's interested. Does it mean anything?"

"Just a few more dots on the timeline," I said. "They can be connected if anyone wants to."

The conversation drifted away from Bickering and the dig. Max had gone quiet. I couldn't tell whether he was thinking or preoccupied with something else.

When we finished eating, April and Marissa cleared the table and I went to the car to bring in the pictures. I had thought of looking at them in the conservatory, but the kitchen would be fine.

I placed the portrait on the table and unfolded the blanket it was wrapped in.

The three of them gathered before it. I stood to the side, wanting to see their expressions.

"It seems that this young lady was in the de Merveilleux family."

I glanced at April to see if she remembered that Marissa had known a girl by that name.

I explained that the pictures hadn't been restored, but only cleaned, and in the case of the portrait, only the area around the pendant had the varnish removed and the small area cleaned.

"You will remember that this used to be a pearl," I said. "Several people thought it looked like an alteration but only when the restorer cleared the over painting that we could see the boar: the emblem of Richard III."

Marissa looked more interested in this picture than she had been by the morning's revelations.

"Wouldn't it have been very dangerous to wear that?" she asked.

"Indeed, it would," I agreed. "I doubt she wore it at all apart for this picture – which would not have left the house, and probably not seen by anyone outside the family. Of course, when de Merveilleux was involved in the Lincolnshire Rising, the game was up and all was lost."

Marissa nodded.

"But the picture appears to have still been in the hall until the fire, years later," she protested.

"So it seems," I said. "I leave it to you to investigate. For what it's worth, I can think of several likely scenarios: first, it might have been in a cupboard or loft space, out of sight. Secondly, the new owner might never have lived in the house and things just stayed as they were. Or, maybe, the local political climate made such a display acceptable – or – here's one to ponder – maybe this lady married the new owner in some deal – to save the lives of family members, perhaps.

"I'm sorry, Max," I said. "This is pure speculation and you'll want evidence. I'm not jumping to conclusions, but setting out some possibilities."

"She deserves a proper frame, " Marissa and April said nearly simultaneously.

Marissa smiled at her mother and nodded.

"She deserves to be hung somewhere."

I wrapped her up and put the flower picture on the table and unwrapped it. This was the one where the cleaning and new varnish had made the biggest difference. The colours leapt from the canvas.

"We kept that in a cupboard?!" April exclaimed. "It looks amazing."

Marissa gaped at it.

"It's more amazing than you think," I said. "This is a religious painting – Catholic painting."

I explained how each of the flowers had an association with the Blessed Virgin.

"What's more is that we know from these flowers that it is English," I said. "The Courtauld really wants you to show these two paintings. They are historically valuable as pieces of art that survived the Tudors' destruction and they are also of great monetary value."

They looked at the painting, picking out the types of flowers and laughing when they discovered the insects.

I wrapped it and replaced it on the table with the pub picture but left it covered.

"Did you print the drone pictures?" I asked Marissa. "Also, can you bring the tablet."

She went to the small study and returned with colour prints of the drone photographs and the tablet.

"This is the least valuable painting, and if it does not solve the mysteries, it provides valuable leads," I said, unfolding the blanket.

"There's nothing on it to suggest who painted it or where it hung," I continued. "The clothing – such as we can see - suggests the early years of the nineteenth century, pre-regency, and I believe it to be a view of Bickering from the windmill."

There was nearly a five second silence before all three started talking at once and pointing at various features. Marissa quickly grasped the significance of the drone picture and held it before the painting.

"*The road was moved,*" Max said. "That's why there's no sign of the hall on the other side of the road, near the priory."

He had a big grin on his face, as he visualised the scene in this new way.

"Marissa and I supposed that it hadn't been as grand a house as supposed and was a wood and plaster affair like Nonsuch Palace," he said, turning to me.

Nonsuch had been a vast but cheaply built building of which virtually nothing survives today. Like Beckford's Fonthill Abbey, it was designed to impress visually, but had the durability of a stage set.

"That's why you had me fly the drone back between the mound and the chapel," Marissa said, finding the beginning of the video clip.

We gathered around the screen and watched as it flew down the lane before veering off to take the route of the old road.

"From the painting, we should be able to find where the old road turned off," she said to Max, then turned to look at her mother. She had gone.

Marissa shrugged.

"Why do you suppose the ruins were covered so quickly?" Max asked. "Was there a change of ownership? Land usage? Or, perhaps taxation? And why was the road moved."

We considered this.

"It might have been a good place for ambushing people," Marissa suggested. "Passing between two derelict sites at night couldn't have been pleasant. All sorts of people could have been living rough in the old chapel."

"Hence the bones," I said.

"Another research topic," Max said.

After wrapping the painting, I went to the car to bring in my watercolours and sketches. They would be anticlimactic after the paintings, but they were what brought me back to Bickering in the first place.

The atmosphere seemed to change as soon as I showed them the first one. It lifted, and smiles broke out on Marissa and Max's faces. They immediately began telling stories about the people and the work.

They leafed through all of them twice, taking nearly half an hour to look at details and point things out. We then looked at all the pencil sketches of the people and they laughed at some of the poses and expressions.

"They will love these," Max said. "It will cement their memories for a very long time."

"I should give them all a full set of prints of the watercolours, too," Marissa said. "Postcard size."

Marissa put her arm around me and leaned on me as we studied all of them again.

It was in this pose that April found us when she re-entered the kitchen.

"I'm glad to see things are going well," she said. "What was causing all the laughter?"

Marissa showed her and shared stories about some of the scenes.

"They're wonderful, Nigel!" Marissa said, enthusiastically. "We should hang them in the hall and invite everyone to come for a party and give them their pictures at the same time. The end of the dig was a bit of a downer, and this would be fun. We'll do it in the summer and can have food on the lawn!"

She turned to her mother who hadn't made any comment, but had a quizzical look on her face.

"What is it, Mother? Are you all right?"

"Yes. I'm fine, dear," April said softly. "It's just that I remembered something when you were looking at the old pictures."

She handed Marissa a small velvet-covered box.

Marissa opened it tentatively, and we all gasped.

In it was a small silver boar.

"You can have it, if you like," April said. "I hate it. Who wants to wear a pig?"

Epilogue

September

I was perfectly content to say goodbye to everyone in Bickering after delivering the pictures. I'd created a lot of work for Max and Marissa should they wish to pursue it.

Needless to say, there was an explosion of discussion after April produced the silver boar. I stayed just long enough to see that the size and shape appeared to be the same as in the portrait, then made my excuses and left.

I stopped at Rachel's cottage where she gave me an antique gold matinée-length *sautoir* with small, brilliant-cut amethysts along its length finishing with a large tear-drop.

"It's the one I was planning to wear with the dress," she said.

I made her take a colour photo, print it and write a short receipt that stated that she had lent the necklace to me, and I had received it. We both signed each copy, and I folded my copy and put it in the case with the necklace.

It was good to be able to see the actual corner that I had painted from Rachel's photos. I could see things that were slightly different, but she had approved it, so I was content.

She gave me a cup of tea before I headed back to the hotel and chatted about school. I told her nothing about Marissa's paintings, watercolours, sketches, the boar, or plans for a party.

Before going, I asked if she had noticed that Bickering Hall had once been owned by the Rawden family and if they were related to the Rawdings.

"That sort of thing would have excited me once," she said. "A little girl fancying herself in a grand house with lots of rooms and servants."

She smiled.

"Of course, it would have been Paul's family if there were a connection, not mine," she continued. "It did catch my eye when I read it, but the hall was not his, it's certainly not mine, and there's nothing there anyway.

"Had he been alive, it might have been fun to trace and joke about, but it could be a completely different family – though most people in Lincolnshire are related, at least in the rural areas."

ca

As planned, Sophie came to the studio a week or so before I needed to get Rachel's portrait and the others to the Royal Academy. We made several attempts at the pose, trying to strike a balance between being natural and showing the necklace to full advantage.

"You don't want the portrait to look like an advertisement for Bulgari," Sophie quipped, and I realised that that was a real danger.

While we fussed with it, Sophie grew thoughtful.

"Has it occurred to you what you're doing?" she asked.

I looked up, puzzled.

"You've just spent the last few months delving into the picture of a young lady wearing a pendant, and now you're painting one."

She paused.

"Is that irony? Déjà vu? Coincidence? Destiny?"

The thought had clearly struck her deeply.

I gave a small laugh.

"Yes, it's partially irony," I said, "but it's also the culmination of all we've done recently: the dig, the paintings, and this portrait."

"So what is it?" she asked, her eyes glistening.

"It's Time talking to us."

Eventually, we got it right and the picture was finished. I took some high resolution pictures of it and emailed them to Rachel. I had three pictures in the Royal Academy Summer Exhibition and two in the one for the Royal Portrait Society. I felt they were all workmanlike but not exceptional.

In late May, *Relative Values* opened its pre-London run to good reviews and full houses. Jackie Streetly had taken over the direction and, according to Sophie, the cast relaxed, and things moved ahead smoothly.

Once the paintings had been delivered, I could turn my focus to the much-delayed introduction to David Powell's book. He had sent me copies of the unpublished essays that would be included in the new book.

After several pretentious ideas, I decided to focus on the difference between an art writer and an art critic, and while thinking about that, I considered that there was something to be said about the difference between public and private art and how that had evolved.

&ȣ;

The summer passed without hearing from Marissa, April or Max. I did get several phone calls from Helena Stirakis.

Sophie and I visited the Royal Academy on a Sunday in June when she didn't have a performance. I was able to walk further and further, but the ankle and leg would tire from lack of use. As usual, the crowds were thick, but she was able to move through it with near anonymity.

I had not gone to any of the opening events – which RAs were encouraged, but not compelled – to attend, so I was seeing the exhibition for the first time, too.

The Yellow Frock hung on the same wall as Sophie's portrait had hung years before. The wall had been painted a rich, creamy colour that set off the dress to maximum effect. Next to the label on the wall with its green "not for sale" sticker, three other notices had been placed announcing that the painting had won *three* of the magazine and newspaper awards. I knew of two of them – Sophie did not – but the third was a surprise.

The reviews in the newspapers had, once again, been kind about my efforts, both at the R.A. and at Mall Galleries, and I had received some new commissions that I was considering.

I went to the exhibition again in July, when it was even busier. This time, I went with Rachel who was anxious about seeing herself in such a public position.

Once the show had opened and the prizes awarded, there was speculation in the popular press about who the woman in *The Yellow Frock* was. Speculation ranged from her being an heiress to my mistress. Rachel found it hard to believe that it could matter to anyone.

"Isn't the painting enough?" she demanded, as we walked through the galleries.

It was a question I'd been asking myself for nearly fifty years.

"Don't those idiots realise that their flippant musings about people in pictures can hurt real people?" she asked, after a perceptive visitor to the R.A. recognised her. The visitor had been perfectly polite, and there was no incident, but it left Rachel in need of a cup of tea and a Florentine at Richoux.

◌ঙ

I was at my studio tidying up on a Monday morning in early September when my buzzer went and I heard Max Hillyard on the intercom. I buzzed him in, and went to meet him at the lift.

He was his usual pleasant self but agitated. I gave him a coffee as he brought me up to date on what he was doing (a Saxon site in Kent). I asked how things were in Bickering.

He gave an ironic laugh.

"All right, I guess," he said. "I haven't been there since the garden party."

I had been invited but begged off.

"They're not doing anything with those paintings, you know," he said. "All that history in three pictures and they won't let anyone see them. They're just hanging in the upstairs hallway. They haven't even had the silver boar looked at."

I had come to accept this.

"For you, it's exasperating," I began, "but you really can't blame them. With the publicity comes higher insurance rates, increased security systems, and being a target for unwanted attention and harassment.

"Those paintings were in a closet for two hundred years for a reason. The reason is different now, but it's no less valid."

Max considered this.

"I know, but – "

"It's not our business, Max," I said, gently. "I see their point. Besides, they'll come to light again one day. You've uncovered the chapel – if that's what it is – and found the ruins of the hall. Marissa might be more interested in excavating that one day. It's no threat to her home."

He thought some more and stared into his mug.

"That's not actually why I came," he said, when he looked up.

"Come to commission a portrait?"

He smiled, then looked straight at me.

"No; I've come to try to buy one. That one."

He pointed at *The Yellow Frock* which was on my easel pending getting it to Rachel.

More than I thought seemed to have happened since I was last in Lincolnshire.

"That's only a copy," I said. "The original is in Bardney."

"You painted two?"

"No, but it's really the original you want, isn't it – and that one can't be bought."

He dropped is gaze and sighed.

"Let me tell you, Dr Hillyard, you stand a better chance of getting the original than you do of getting this one."

"I wish."

"How hard have you tried?" I asked.

"She's got that detective chasing her," he said, miserably.

"She'd understand a detective, and it would be familiar," I conceded, "but do you really think she wants a reminder of Paul living with her?"

"You think?"

"What have you got to lose, young man?" I said encouragingly. "You seem to be pretty miserable now, and there's a chance you might not be after you call her up."

He brightened.

"I'll drop in."

"Call her first. Neither of you will want to destroy the images you have in your minds."

∽

Sophie, of course, told me that I'd said all the wrong things and proceeded to tell me the right things.

"Not to provoke a war, but that's not the advice men give to each other," I said, after listening to her.

At least she laughed.

We'd gone out to dinner and were back in Sophie's set enjoying the rest of the bottle that we'd started before dinner.

"I'm thinking of retiring," I said, breaking the news to her for the first time. "It's been a good year, and producing a multiple-prize winner like *The Frock* isn't going to happen again."

She put her wine glass down and turned towards me. "You *what*?"

Her vehemence surprised me.

"I can't go on working forever," I said.

"You need to keep working until you're walking to the studio both ways!"

That was true. I was walking one way – usually to the studio – and taking the Underground or a taxi back.

"Anyway, what would you do all day? I don't want you turning into another of Albany's ghosts. There are enough already."

I laughed.

"It's either that or you drown in gin and tonic at your club! I don't want people to remember you for that, darling."

She was still cross at the idea.

"You still have talent and should use it," Sophie said, giving it her award-winning emotive power. "What's more, you believe that God gave it to you, so use it until the tube is squeezed empty."

She was right. I liked the idea of retiring; what I didn't like was the idea of stopping painting.

"Listen, darling, my dear friend: I have nothing on until mid-October," she said. "Let's go to Rhodes, or Marrakech or Salamanca for a few weeks – you always wanted to go there.

"Or we could go to Rome and you could reinvent yourself as a religious painter."

Acknowledgements, Notes & References

Ian Thomson, novelist and teacher, for his knowledge of and enthusiasm for Lincoln and Lincolnshire.

Julie Dexter, editor, proof reader and critic, who on the beaches of Hawaii, still finds time to correct and advise.

The following notes and references are to help readers find more information about various topics mentioned.

Just as the Oval Office is often portrayed in films as being in the upper story of the south façade of the White House, I have placed the conservation department of the Courtauld Institute of Art in Somerset House for two reasons. First, it will be more familiar to readers, and secondly, it is easier for Sir Nigel to walk to. It is, of course, at the Courtauld's Vernon Square (WC1) site.

Diarmaid MacCulloch, "The Devastation of British Art", BBC Radio 3, October 2013

Lawrence Shafe, "The Wholesale Destruction of English Art"

Father Dwight Longenecker, "Catholic England on the Eve of Destruction by the English Reformation," Catholic Education Resource Centre, 2017.

Sophie Hacker, artist, for her interesting thoughts on modern ecclesiastical art. Found at sophiehacker.com and many other websites.

Richard Williams, Professor of Contemporary Visual Cultures, History of Art , Edinburgh College of Art, University of Edinburgh.

Dominic Selwood, "Thomas Cromwell was the Islamic State of his day," *The Telegraph*, Saturday, January 24, 2015.

Timothy C.G. Rich, "List of vascular plants endemic to Britain, Ireland and the Channel Islands 2020" *British & Irish Botany* 2(3): 169-189.

Lindsay, Nicholas, "Hamiltonian circle actions on complete intersections," *Journal of the London Mathematical Society*, Vol. 54, Issue 1, March 2022.

Numrich Gun Parts Corporation, Kingston, New York https://www.gunpartscorp.com/gun-manufacturer/colt/black-pow-revolvers/1851-navy

Forensic archaeology: Finding human bones https://www.futurelearn.com/info/courses/forensic-archaeology-and-anthropology/0/steps/67861

The Weather Project
https://www.youtube.com/watch?v=IsT9vEpfNq4 This short video captures the atmosphere, serenity and engagement of this piece and helps to preserve the experience of seeing it.

Ai Weiwei's *Sunflower Seeds* is given good exposure in the video of the press preview: https://www.youtube.com/watch?v=td3_EKX1Igo The problematic ceramic dust can be easily seen.

"Revealed - the 100-plus medieval Lincolnshire villages that were wiped off the map"
https://www.lincolnshirelive.co.uk/news/local-news/revealed-100-plus-medieval-lincolnshire-3463235

"Lost Houses of Lincolnshire"
http://www.lostheritage.org.uk/lh_complete_list.html

"Lincolnshire's lost medieval villages"
https://www.lincolnshirelive.co.uk/news/local-news/revealed-100-plus-medieval-lincolnshire-3463235

By the same author:

The Trumbull Chronicles

Fourscore and Upward
The Time of No Horizon
In an Age without Honor

Stories

Undivulged Crimes
Thoughts and Whispers
Clubs, Bills and Partisans

Novels

Circle of Vanity
Ardmore Endings
The Rock Pool
Lost Lady
On the Edge of Dreams and Nightmares
The Countess Comes Home
Entrusted in Confidence
Portland Place: A novel of the time of Jane Austen
The Camels of the Qur'an
Wachusett
Nantucket Summer

Lattimer & Co.

Lattimer & Co. was established in Philadelphia in 1870 by "Colonel" Jonas Lattimer. The company now includes the imprints of Defarge Frères and Éditions Chaillot, both of Paris.

Printed in Great Britain
by Amazon

42817875R00199